In the Midst of Wolves

In the Midst of Wolves

KAREN KELLY BOYCE

In the Midst of Wolves

First printing, 2014

Copyright © 2014 by Karen Kelly Boyce

Cover art copyright © by Andrew Gioulis
Cover design copyright © by Sue Andrew Gioulis
Book design by Andrew Gioulis

Photographs of the author copyright © Andrew Gioulis.
Used by permission.

All rights reserved.
No part of this book may be reproduced in any form without the written permission of the publisher.

Published by: KFR Communications, LLC
1024 Old Corlies Avenue
Neptune, NJ 07753

Publisher's Note: The author and publisher have taken care in preparation of this book but make no expressed or implied warranty of any kind and assume no responsibility for errors or omissions. No liability is assumed for incidental or consequential damages in connection with or arising out of the use of the information contained herein.

ISBN-10: 1939406102
ISBN-13: 978-1-939406-10-1

Printed in the United States of America

www.kfrcommunications.com

Dedicated to my friend and fellow author
Karen F. Riley.

She loved.

1962–2013

1 Corinthians: 13

Behold, I send you forth as sheep in the midst of wolves; be ye therefore wise as serpents, and harmless as doves.

Matt. 10: 16

The Fourth Joyful mystery - The Presentation

The Grace of the Mystery

Purity

Contents

Chapter One 9

Chapter Two 19

Chapter Three 27

Chapter Four 35

Chapter Five 43

Chapter Six 51

Chapter Seven 57

Chapter Eight 65

Chapter Nine 75

Chapter Ten 83

Chapter Eleven 89

Chapter Twelve 97

Chapter Thirteen 105

Chapter Fourteen 111

Chapter Fifteen 121

Chapter Sixteen 129

Chapter Seventeen 137

Chapter Eighteen 145

Chapter Nineteen 153

Chapter Twenty 161

Chapter Twenty One 169

ABOUT THE AUTHOR 177

Too Much Good
by Karen Kelly Boyce

I always thought they didn't know
The men with torch and sword
That the God who prayed in the garden night
Was the same who walked in Eden's light.
Until I read He said "I AM" and they
Fell right to the ground
It hit me hard to realize that they knew
it was God bound.

It seems men like a little light—
A little light just shines.
The light of God is so complete
It burns up things men
Want to keep.

It seems men like a little good
A little good is fine
The good of God is much too much
It takes things that are mine.
And so men nod as Mother leaves—
Yet beat their chest for Di.

The Good of God made Francis poor to
Dance the hills of joy
And roses fell from heaven above

To mark the little way of love.
Teresa walked the castle steps—
As men watched from the moat
But truth be told, they like removed
The thought of saints who float.

The men who followed Judas came
They came because they knew
It was too much for Good to walk,
It Shone too bright to hear God talk.
With ignorant pride, men trample and trod—
With Hands of nail and wood
And enter into the garden of God,
To kill the Shine of Too Much Good.

Oh God—the truth it burns so bright
The Shine, it burns my eyes.
My smugness in my easy gift
Pride in the shine of I
How often have I come at night
With hands of nail and wood—
To crucify the gift of God,
The Shine of Too Much Good?

Prologue

We frantically spend our lives accumulating power, fame, or money. Yet, we spend life's true wealth and give it away without thought. As our life progresses we notice that the days, seasons, and years seem to be accelerating. It is not until our later days, when we are running low, that we realize what is slipping through our fingers. Suddenly, the truth of what we have wasted hits us. It is not about fame, money, or power. These are not important in the end. For in the end we find that the true wealth and currency of life is time.

Time dripped—slow as the leak in the bathroom sink. Her thoughts poured between the drops. *Ah…but it has always been so,* she mused. Often, she couldn't catch up with her own mind. Certainly no one else could. Regina Kagan had learned early not to allow others to see the quickening pace of her heart or the narrowing of her yellow eyes. Regina presented a calm, serene countenance. Appearing beyond the reach of ordinary worries, she sat in the plastic chair of the hospital waiting room. She was a watcher, an observer of human nature. The gift of understanding human nature was one of the many abilities that had propelled her into the lifestyle she enjoyed. Early on, she had noticed the small expressions and movements of people. She learned to read the tiny quiver of the lip, the downward glance of eyes. Regina noticed almost unperceivable movements which revealed the hidden thoughts of those around her. When she was a child, these skills had been necessary for her survival. Now that she was an adult, they always gave her the advantage.

Watching closely, she noticed the furrowed brow of her son-in-law. She heard his deep sighs as his eyes darted, settling on nothing. Regina watched him as a wild animal observes prey while hidden behind the bush. She knew the fear that drove the expressions. It annoyed her to watch his lack of control, his feeling of helplessness. *I would never allow myself to feel so vulnerable,* she thought as she watched him pace restlessly around the waiting room.

"Mr. Laverty?" the nurse called. "You can come in now to see your wife. It was very close—we had to rush her from the E.R. straight into the delivery room."

Regina's eyes followed as he hurried out of the lounge. He was being called to the delivery room. Her daughter lay beyond the walls. *But not beyond my reach,* she thought. Regina had made sure that she handpicked Bridget's obstetrician. Thinking ahead as always, she had found a young doctor who was under pressure. The doctor was a young man with a large amount of ambition and little money. *People who want things are always so easy to control,* she thought. Regina needed control. She had paid off the young doctor's onerous student loans. She smiled to herself thinking, *John may be in the delivery room, but my presence there is stronger.*

Whether she would need that advantage, she didn't know. She had learned early never to be without it. Fidgeting, she couldn't ease the ache in her back that betrayed her age. *These molded chairs are so uncomfortable,* she thought. The chairs weren't made for those with backs that curved with the weight of age. Regina hated her weakening body. She had done everything she could to outrun death—but it grew closer with every day. She had accomplished so much in the fifty-five years she had lived. *I've built an empire,* she thought as the memories of fighting her way to the top comforted her. She was the richest woman in the state and owed her success to no one but herself. She had beaten all who dared to get in her way. She always won.

I failed at only one thing, she sighed as she raised her shoulders in an attempt to ease the pain in the base of her back. Somewhere along the way she had lost control of her daughter Bridget. It had surprised her when her daughter married against her will—married a poor teacher, instead of forming the wealthy alliance that Regina planned. The final confrontation between Bridget and herself was seared in her memory. She could still picture it. Bridget stood tall on the landing of the staircase in the foyer of Regina's mansion. Trembling, she stated that she was leaving and no one could stop her. Regina had tried. She had physically leapt—blocking Bridget's way. Yet, she had lost. The burning look of resolve and determination in Bridget's eyes had melted her. She moved to get out of her daughter's way. She felt as if she had shriveled that morning—shrunk in defeat. It was the look on Bridget's face that had defeated her

Bridget, so soft, kind, and compliant, had stared at her with a face so full of disdain that Regina's will dissolved. For the first time in her life, Regina had felt exposed, as if Bridget could see the real her. In the light of truth, the truth of what she was—she had withered. Small, she had watched as Bridget left. *Never again! It will never happen again!* her mind screamed as she tossed herself around in the chair. Regina had a second chance and no one was going to take it away from her.

*

John stood awkwardly, shifting from one foot to the other. He stood at the head of the gurney as his wife lay before him. She was lightly sedated and seemingly unaware of the machines that buzzed and whirled around her. John felt useless in the foreign setting. Everyone moved purposely around, busy with tasks that confused him. The masked attendants took little notice of him as they arranged for the birth of his son. To the medical staff the preparations seemed routine, mundane. Bridget was covered with sheets, and John was screened from the actual birth of his son. Bridget moaned and quivered below him as the staff encouraged her to bear down. With her hair matted and her pain whispered into the air, Bridget obeyed. The nurses were jubilant.

"Look at that head of hair! He's a red-head!" they said as the baby tried to clear his shoulders through the birth canal. It was a scene of expectant joy that John would always remember—remember because it was a joy of short duration.

Lusty cries filled the air, as the angry babe protested his birth. Clearing his shoulders, he slipped into his new world. As the nurse started to lift him away, she gasped, startled, "What is wrapped around his ankle?"

"It's a hand! There's another baby!" the circulating nurse said to the doctor who had already turned away, thinking his job just about done. The small hand clasped tightly to the newborn's ankle. The delivery nurse had to pry it loose to free the baby already born. The tiny twin slipped weakly out. Just half the size of his brother, the undersized fetus proclaimed his presence with soft mews like a half-dead kitten. Making frantic calls, the circulating nurse summoned help. The neonatal nurse arrived with an Isolette and whisked the second baby to the neonatal care unit.

"Looks like unequal twins!" stated the doctor as the nurse wiped the perspiration from his brow. As the first born was being weighed and measured, the doctor finished with the aftermath of birth and again rose to leave. The monitor screeched as the mother's blood pressure soared. Again, the doctor was stopped by the unexpected.

"She's stroking out! Code blue!" shouted the circulating nurse as she grabbed the code cart and wheeled it to the head of the gurney.

Another nurse took the father's arm and firmly guided him out of the room. "Don't worry. We will do everything we can."

John's hands shook as he stood in the hallway. His senses dulled. The scene before him seemed surreal. With a faint sense of queasiness, he watched as a cart, loaded with equipment, was pushed into the delivery room. The wheels of the cart squealed as it made a sharp turn into the room. He could hear the sound of drawers slamming as the doctor barked orders to the nurses. One professional after another arrived and rushed to his wife's room. Uniformed people flowed out of the elevator and filled the delivery room. The crowd of caregivers spilled out into the hallway, blocking his view of his wife.

John swallowed hard, his worried mind unable to comprehend the actions that played out before him. The immensity of his fear became unbearable. As if to cushion the pain, his mind, unsure of what was happening in the present, filled with memories. He could remember Bridget laughing in the morning light. She had been bursting with joy as the impending birth of her first born approached. She had filled the last few months with shopping sprees for baby clothes. She spent hours decorating the small nursery next to their bedroom. Visions of Bridget painting the walls a pale yellow were replaced by images of the numerous stuffed animals that covered the rocking chair beside the crib. Quiet joy had flowed through the air of their first home as the promise of new life softened the face of the wife he loved so.

What is happening? First a twin—now this! My God, don't let her die! John's mind screamed. The hurried pace of the emergency lasted only fifteen minutes but fear stretched each moment into what seemed a lifetime. Finally, John could hear the monitor beat at a steady rhythm as the crowd thinned and retreated back into the hidden bowels of the hospital. He didn't like the look of resignation on the doctor's face as he approached.

"What's happened? Is Bridget all right?" John's voice shook as the doctor put his hand on John's shoulder.

"She's had a C.V.A.—a stroke. We're moving her to the I.C.U. Only time will tell how much damage there is. Why don't you go see your new sons? It will be a while before you can see Bridget." The doctor turned to follow his patient to the unit.

John watched as his wife's stretcher was wheeled to the elevator. As the doors to the elevator closed, he looked down at his hands. *I can't help her!* he thought. He obeyed the doctor. He could feel his hands tremble as he walked to the nursery to see his newborn sons.

Standing before the neonatal intensive care unit, John watched as the nurses applied leads to the tiny baby. *That wrinkled skin and shrunken face makes him look more like an elderly man than a baby,* he thought, hating himself for thinking it. *Or like a hairless rat.* Feeling a presence beside him, he turned to see his mother-in-law.

"That's the second twin, the unexpected one," John stated without emotion.

Regina lifted her head and inhaled through her nose, as if smelling something bad.

"Humph!" was her only answer as she walked quickly toward the normal nursery. John quietly followed. He had learned long ago never to question this woman. He followed, softly stepping behind her soldier-like march. Then he stood beside her as she gazed into the nursery window.

*

It only took Regina a moment to find her grandson amidst the numerous nursery residents. There he was—large and strong with a shock of red hair that made him stand out. As the nurse lifted him and carried him to the window, he struggled to open his eyes, still sensitive to the light of this new world.

Regina's heart jumped as she looked at him. So new and strong! He let out a cry: not a wimpy cry, but a cry of strength. It was her grandson announcing his presence. Suddenly, as if he could transfer his health and strength, Regina felt a force growing within her. She felt young. The aches in her back seemed to fade. A sense of power and life flowed through her body. *This is it,* Regina's heart whispered. *He is what I need to live for.*

*

John watched his mother-in-law. He would never understand her. She stared at the newborn like she was looking at a meal. With glowing eyes she licked her lips, as if ready to devour the baby. Grinning, she just turned and without a word walked away. *She hasn't asked about Bridget at all,* John realized.

See, upon the palms of my hands I have written your name.
—Isaiah 49: 16

Chapter One

There is an ancient legend that explains how a child receives his name. According to the legend, when a mother is about to give birth, angels are sent from heaven to whisper the child's name into the parent's ear. Thus the name, if properly given, is bestowed by the Creator according to the child's destiny.

Names reflect more than the fashion of the day. Although some names may be hard to trace, each name has a source, a meaning. I once knew a woman who did research into the meaning of names. She would entertain crowds by stringing each person's names together, forming sentences. It is startling how often the original connotation of a person's name is a true revelation of who they are. Perhaps, when we are lost or confused we can find ourselves by naming who we are.

John spent each day for a month by Bridget's bedside. He grew weary sitting in a vinyl chair, reading and talking to her. Each day he arrived with renewed hope but she remained non-responsive. Daily E.E.G.'s were taken to access her brain function. He prayed, with each test, hoping she was not brain-dead. His eyes filled with tears as he watched the pump of the respirator rising and falling, breathing for Bridget. At times he would kiss her forehead tenderly, but at other times he wanted to shake her. *Will she ever wake up*, he thought. Her eyes remained closed. John wondered if she was aware of her surroundings. He had heard some of the nurses' talk. They didn't expect her to recover. His heart froze when he heard their doom-filled whispers.

The doctor seemed more optimistic. As the days stretched on, John watched in horror as the man next to Bridget, hidden behind curtains, lost his battle to live. John had grown to admire the loving care given by the man's three daughters. *Is this what's going to happen to me,* he wondered. His heart surged with pain as the daughters clung to each other and wept.

Unable to sit still and listen to the crying behind the thin curtain, John left the I.C.U. and wandered the halls of the hospital. He felt numb as he noticed the door to the hospital chapel. Pushing open the door, he found an empty room. Painted a bland white, the small room had three rows of pine pews. The pews faced a stained glass window that displayed a red rose with a thorn on its stem. *I guess the chapel is supposed to fit any faith,* John thought as he took a seat in the first pew. He was alone and taken by the classical music that was being softly piped into the chapel. It was supposed to give comfort, but it angered John.

Am I supposed to sit here and forget that God allowed this to happen! His mind screamed within him. His face flushed as the heat of his anger rose to the surface. *Where are you now! Why don't you help me?* his mind cried to the red rose. Bending over, with his elbows on his knees, John covered his face with both hands. *I don't need a red rose,* he cried, *I need the real God!*

He could feel the tears that he had been holding back gush from his eyes. Sitting alone in the chapel, John cried until his tears ran dry. He had an image of Jesus on the crucifix, looking silently at him. *Why? Why did this have to happen?* He asked the suffering image of Jesus. *Don't let her die,* he begged. Still the image remained – silent and beckoning. It didn't speak or move. Instead it just remained. Eternal and comforting, it stayed in his mind. When all the pain he had inside had been poured out, John sat up, removing his hands from his face. He opened his eyes, but the sight of the rose startled him. There was a single drop of red that seemed to be falling from the rose.

I didn't notice that before, he thought, *it looks like blood.* Suffering, it seemed so hard to understand the why of suffering. *But is it for me to understand,* he thought. A sense of peace came over him. It washed over him like a warm ocean wave. *Bridget belongs to God. It's not for me to understand, I'm not God,* he realized. *Lord, I give her to you,* he spoke within his soul...*Our Father*...he began.

His daily routine became robotic. With little sleep his eyes grew red with weariness. His face was drawn and thinning. *I haven't had a hot meal in weeks,* John realized as he mindlessly swallowed another snack from the vending machine. Each day bled into the next. The hospital was a world unto itself. It had its own rules and its own sense of time.

John was lost in I.C.U. time—the day cut into two twelve-hour shifts, the windowless unit without sun to distinguish the day from the night. His care for his wife kept him from his sons. The older twin remained at the home of his mother-in-law. Regina Kagan took control of all his needs, making all the arrangements for his future. The small, dark-haired twin joined his brother two weeks later, released from the hospital's care.

Three weeks after the stroke, John was sitting beside Bridget when she opened her eyes for the first time. She thrashed around the bed, confused, unable to understand where she was. Seeing John right beside her seemed to comfort her.

"Shh...Bridget, you're in the hospital. Rest, you're on the mend," John whispered as he stroked her arm.

The next morning, she was removed from life-support, apparently breathing on her own. She choked and coughed as the nurse pulled the intubation tube from her throat.

Taking a deep breath, Bridget asked, "Where is my baby?"

Her mind asked about the baby—the words her mouth pronounced were, "Blue chair." Bridget couldn't believe the words she heard.

Holding her throat, she began again, "Blue chair, blue chair."

"Do you want to get out of bed?" John asked.

Bridget's face reddened.

No! Her mind screamed in frustration.

"Yes," she heard herself answer.

"Now, now honey, you're not ready to get out of bed yet!" answered the nurse.

Angry, Bridget yelled, *Shut up!*

"Turkey" was the word she pronounced.

Tilting her head, the nurse turned to John, "Something's not right. I'll call the doctor and let him know."

Bridget wanted to scream, *Just listen!*

Instead she screamed incoherently, "door fell."

The doctor appeared within the hour, and confirmed the diagnosis of aphasia. Bridget couldn't talk.

"This will pass." The doctor said, "As the swelling of the brain recedes."

Bridget, now on the mend, was wheeled out of the unit to a regular floor. As the days wore on, her physical health improved. The nurses got her up to a chair and physical therapy taught her to walk again. However, her words didn't make sense despite numerous visits by speech therapy.

Bridget strained to speak—broken nonsense spilling from her lips. John tried to anticipate her questions, telling her of the twins and how they were doing. He barely knew himself, since his contact with them was limited. It consisted of short peeks into the nursery before he collapsed exhausted into bed each night. The dawn would find him on the road to the hospital before the twins awoke. Yet, the visits to his wife had become more difficult with every day. Bridget's anger over her inability to communicate had mushroomed over the last week. She grew frustrated, punching the bed with her fist as if the punctuation would give her jumbled words the meaning they should have.

Those around her began to dismiss her attempts. Nurses talked to her as if she were a child, telling her what she needed. Visitors left quickly, uncomfortable with her grunts and muddled expressions. John remained by her bedside, patiently trying to unravel her vocabulary with little luck. Bridget grew more and more irritated. Tears streaked her face as she grew increasingly frustrated with her inability to convey her needs. The angrier she grew, the more the nurses ignored her calls. As the fury crested and finally died, so did her attempts to speak. By the time she was brought home—to her mother's house—she had stopped trying. Bridget became mute.

John felt uncomfortable staying in Regina's home. Regina had demanded the move. *I just can't take her on,* he thought. *I have to concentrate on Bridget's needs.* But in his heart he knew better. He saw the angry look that Bridget gave him when the car pulled up to her childhood home. Bridget grabbed the back of the seat so tightly that the hired nurse had to physically pry her fingers loose to get her out of the car. She sighed as they wheeled her through the front door. John noticed her pain filled expression but ignored the obvious. Regina had always bullied him, and he felt that he was in no position to fight her now. *Besides, she always wins,* he thought, *It's just easier to give in.* Placed in a wheelchair and propelled through the front door by the nurse, Bridget refused to look at John.

In her silence, she allowed herself to be returned to her childhood room, a room she hated, full of lonely memories. It was the room she had successfully escaped with her marriage to John. Pink walls and old stuffed animals soon became her only companions as life proceeded without her. In the morning she would be placed in a chair by the window. After being fed breakfast by the hired nurse, she would gaze out the window watching the sun span the sky. Her only relief was her husband's visits after work, his devotion unending. When he came she would try to speak.

Her mind shouted, *Get me out of here!*

Over and over again, she would hear her voice repeat, "Circus man."

After a while, John would laugh and answer, "Yes, I feel like I work at a circus."

John would spend an hour each afternoon telling her about his day. He sat beside her late into the evening. He was working long hours trying to catch up with his students because of all the time he missed while Bridget was in the hospital. After he left her, John would spend the rest of the evening grading his students' papers. Before he left for his room each night he would bring the babies for her to hold, but as she withdrew to a world within herself, she showed no interest in her sons. Trapped under a blanket of silence, she found little comfort in the outside world. And as she withdrew—the world seemed to lose interest in her.

In contrast, the twins demanded attention, the larger twin with lusty cries of hunger, the dark one with kitten-like whining. A nanny, hired by Regina, attended to all their physical needs. Regina visited the nursery at every chance.

Sweeping in like a mighty wind, she would push past the dark-haired twin's crib to the crib of the red-head. Lifting him up into the air, she delighted in his squeals and smiles as she cooed to him.

"So big and strong you are," she announced. "You're going to be a big, handsome man some day!"

At first the nanny would try to present the smaller twin to Regina. She would bathe the fussy boy and wrap him tightly in a receiving blanket to calm him. It only took a few attempts before she knew that the grandmother wasn't interested in this child. On the third attempt to place the tiny infant in the grandmother's arms, Regina shouted, "Get that puking excuse for a child out of my face." Pushing the small boy, held in the nanny's arms away, she turned to the red-head and cooed, "Here's my real grandson!"

The nanny tried to give the little baby the attention that he didn't seem to receive from his family. It didn't last long. One morning as she was rocking the infant, trying to calm him, Regina found the older twin with a wet diaper.

"What is this!" the grandmother's face reddened with rage, "Put that brat down and take care of my child!" Hannah, the nanny, couldn't help but notice that the grandmother referred to the other twin as her own child, but she put the dark-haired infant down and obeyed the angry woman. She needed this job and the rebukes she received from Regina were severe. Regina wanted all of the nanny's attention to be devoted to the other twin. Hannah stopped her attempts to comfort the tiny infant. The neglected baby had all his physical needs met, but little if no attention.

After a while, Hannah noticed gratefully that the little twin stopped whining. He learned to entertain himself. He grew silent, as silent as his mother in the room across the hall.

John saw little of Regina as his students' papers filled his life, and his visits to Bridget rounded out his day. Therefore, it was an unusual evening when he found himself sitting with Regina at the dinner table. He had not spoken to her for weeks.

"I think that Bridget and I should be going back home soon. She seems to be stable if not fully recovered. She might recover better in her own home," John stated weakly.

Regina took a moment of silence to emphasize her response. "That's very selfish of you. Don't you think that being with her mother and having the best medical care in the world will get her well?"

"She can have a nurse at our house until she is fully recovered," gulped John. His mother-in-law was a powerful force.

"Oh, and that nurse will have to divide her attention between the twins and Bridget. I don't think so. She is better off here!" Regina retorted.

"Okay, I guess we shouldn't move her now," John murmured.

Regina smiled and decided with the taste of victory to change the subject. "You do know that the babies need to be baptized. Do you want me to make the arrangements?" asked Regina, although she had already called the church.

"I guess, I haven't really given it much thought." John paused, and then continued. "I know that Bridget had picked out a first and middle name for one son. She didn't expect two. I guess we should give each boy one of the names she picked."

A flash of anger passed over Regina's face, but John, reaching for his drink, didn't notice.

Regina, now composed and smiling, asked, "And what names did she mention?"

"She had already decided to call him Benedict Flynn," John answered.

"All right," Regina nodded. "I'll make the arrangements for the baptism. I hope you don't mind since Bridget is sick and you are so busy."

John stared at his mother-in-law. "All right, just make sure that each boy receives one of the names that Bridget wanted."

"Oh, don't worry, I'll make sure—Benedict and Flynn," she smiled.

*

It was an early summer Sunday when the boys were dressed for their baptism. Satin and lace wrapped the twins in celebration. The hired nurse dressed Bridget and led her to the car. Silently she sat with no response to the wails of her children. Yet with every coo and cry her body, so seemingly detached from her mind, tensed. Her muscles tightened, making her look stiff and uncertain. Settled in the front pew of the church, Bridget stared ahead, as if in deep prayer. No one seemed to notice as strangers cooed over the babies. Godparents, business acquaintances of Regina's, held each baby in turn as water initiated them into their Christian lives. In a loud booming voice worthy of a Broadway actor, the priest spoke each child's acceptance into the Church.

"In the Name of the Father, and of the Son, and of the Holy Spirit, I baptize you, Lander Flynn," the priest proclaimed.

John shifted uncomfortably in his seat. *I should have known that she would pull something,* he thought, resigning himself to the inevitability of Regina's will. The priest held the squirming red-head up to the large Crucifix that dominated the wall behind the altar, as if Jesus would reach down and snatch the child directly into his kingdom.

Holding the smaller twin he poured the font water over his head.

"In the Name of the Father, and of the Son, and of the Holy Spirit, I baptize you, Lowell Benedict," announced the priest as he repeated the ceremony. John shook his head in disgust as he saw the look of triumph on Regina's face. The priest held the tiny infant up to the crucifix which produced a weak whine of protest from the younger twin.

No one noticed the movement of Bridget's lips. She breathlessly tried to form a "no" without success. Silently, a single tear escaped her eye.

> *"Your eyes saw my substance, being yet unformed, and in Your book they all were written, the days fashioned for me, when as yet there were none of them."*
> —Psalm 139: 16

Chapter Two

When we are young we imagine who we will become and what our life is to be. From the time of our childhood we make plans to fulfill the dreams that lie dormant within our hearts. However, life often seems to have its own plans. Life takes twists and turns that lead us on an unplanned journey. With our own wishes tucked away in our pockets we button our spiritual coat and trudge through the storms of reality. We follow fate.

Hannah's life took just such a turn when her physical desires overtook her plans. One night in the back of a car with just a little too much to drink she gave in to a temporary desire and discovered that all her childhood dreams had disappeared with her virginity. She had always imagined herself as a teacher. She wanted to work with children, other people's children. Life took a turn and now she had to make plans for her own child. She had gotten a job as a nanny. The job of caring for the twins was procured by her mother's friend. She thought she could save the money she needed to start community college in the fall. Now as she listened to the raised voices in the next room, she realized that even her new plans were in danger of being changed.

"I won't have a harlot raising my grandson—I want her gone!" Regina screamed. She knew that girl was listening. Maybe if she screamed loud enough, the girl would leave of her own accord.

John's face paled. He dreaded dealing with Regina. He decided to be calm and wait it out. "I'll need some time to find another nanny.

Give me some time, maybe Bridget will get well soon," he answered in a calm, deliberate voice. John Laverty's brow broke out in a light sweat. Staring at the floor, he fidgeted with his watch. *It's always best to placate her*, he thought.

*I'll get rid of that girl late*r, Regina decided. She would just bide her time. She decided that with enough time she could make Hannah leave on her own.

John could see by her reaction that he had won a temporary victory. Hannah would stay. The toddler boys loved her and there was no reason she couldn't care for her own child as she cared for his. The thought of putting a young pregnant girl out on the street was repugnant to him. It was unthinkable.

The playroom next-door to the boy's bedroom was a wonder. Large and colorful, it was lined with shelves that held countless treasures. All the latest toys that were suited for toddlers filled the bottom shelves. Blocks and Lincoln logs, robots and action figures, stuffed dogs and trucks, stared out into the rectangular room waiting to be chosen. The upper shelves held toys and games that the twins would grow into. Their grandmother couldn't seem to wait for them to grow into the magic. There were duplicates of each toy. A shining tile floor held identical handcrafted rocking horses and electric trains. On the other side of the room a large rocking chair purchased with Bridget in mind stood empty and still. There was nothing the boys could desire that they didn't possess. All around the colorfully painted room, it was only the empty rocker that hinted at loss.

Lander screamed with delight as the blocks he had been stacking fell and splayed across the nursery floor. Hannah turned and smiled, for now at least she wouldn't have to leave the boys she had learned to love. Lowell sat silent, paying little attention to the game that Lander played.

How can twins be so different? Hannah wondered as she smiled at the two toddlers. *Now there will be a new baby to raise*, she thought. Suddenly her heart felt peace. For now, at least, she knew her baby would be safe.

Hannah watched thoughtfully as Lander piled up a tower of blocks only to knock them down again. His giggles filled the room with joy as he started to build all over again. Lowell sat quietly—gently rolling a plastic car back and forward as if distracted. His mind didn't seem to be connected with the repetitive motion of his play. *What different personalities! I wonder what my child will be like,* Hannah speculated as she bent to pick up some scattered toys. Hearing the door open, she turned from her thoughts of the future to the present.

"Hello, my boys!" announced John as he crouched and held out his arms to catch Lander.

Lander squealed with delight and ran joyfully into his father's arms while Lowell never even turned to see who had entered. Hannah watched as John, hugging Lander close, looked curiously over Lander's shoulder at the son who ignored him. She saw the fear in his eyes. She held the same fear. *Why did Lowell seem so withdrawn?* The tall brunette walked over to the child and picked him up.

"Lowell, your daddy's here," she whispered in his ear. The child wrapped his arms around her neck and clung tightly. Hannah hugged him back as she walked over to John.

"I'd like to take them to see their mother," John said as he stood up—still holding Lander.

"Do you need my help?" she asked.

"No, why don't you take a break. You need your rest," answered John as he scooped Lowell out of Hannah's arms and carried both boys into the hall.

She watched as Lander giggled and Lowell stiffened with fear.

*

John pulled a chair close to Bridget as the boys stood before their mother. She sat in her usual position—just staring out the window as if no one was in the room.

How long can I stand this loneliness, he mused as he tried to get his wife to turn to him. There was, as usual, no response. It had been two years since the stroke and still Bridget refused to connect with him or the rest of her life. Last year, on the night he received the 'Teacher of the Year' award he had rushed to her room. Excited he wanted to share the honor with the woman he loved.

"Bridget!" he had announced, "Can you believe that I won. The students voted for me! I was shocked when I received the nomination, but to receive the award is beyond my expectations! Now I have a good chance to get tenure and a pay raise."

Disappointed, he looked for a response. Bridget didn't even look his way. She was lost, lost in a world that didn't seem to have room for him or the boys.

Each night, he went to bed alone, tossing and turning. He would hug his pillow just to feel a connection to something. Lying awake he tried to hold back the tears as the sense of separation from the woman he loved overwhelmed him. He had no one to share his dreams or concerns, no one to care. Each night he came to her room after work and talked to a woman who didn't respond. He prayed for a breakthrough. He tried to be funny—to make her laugh as she used to. He tried gossiping about people they both knew to spark her interest. For hours he would sit telling her about his students, and the latest antics of the teacher's lounge. He filled her in on the progress of the twins. Still, she sat staring out the window as if he weren't even there. No matter what he said there was no sign of awareness. Nothing he tried seemed to work.

At first he was full of understanding and sympathy, knowing she must be withdrawn because of depression. He called so many doctors. Specialists came and spent hours with Bridget. Each physician raised his hope with a new anti-depressive drug or treatment. However, each proved to be just a temporary hope. Drug after drug failed. Treatment after treatment proved to be ineffectual. Bridget never changed. Day after day, he walked away alone and discouraged, wondering if she even knew who he was. Today was no different. John talked as the boys played on the floor beside his chair. For an hour he talked about his day with no sign that Bridget was even hearing what he was saying. Shaking his head, he sighed and turned his attention to his sons.

"Lander, Lowell, come and say hello to your mother." John said. Lowell continued to play on the floor, ignoring his father's instructions. Lander smiled widely and clapping his hands rose from the floor.

Grabbing at her clothing, Lander climbed up the distracted woman's leg.

"Mommy, Mommy," he called. Lander refused to accept her apathy as he climbed precariously up to Bridget's lap and put his arms around her waist. She continued to ignore him, staring out the window. Lander reached up and placing his hands on each cheek physically turned her face from the window until she looked down at him. Excited, he let go of his grip and jumped up and down on her lap, joyfully kissing her over and over. Lines deepened between her brows as if she were puzzled by the interruption. Lander bounced unaware of the expression on his mother's face. With his arms clinging to Bridget's neck, Lander jumped up and down, demanding his mother's attention. John couldn't help but laugh as Lander showered his mother with kisses.

It all happened so quickly. Lander let go of his grip and lost his balance as he landed both feet on his mother's lap. Flying high into the air, he fell backwards. John reached out but not quickly enough as Lander's body fell to the floor. A loud cracking sound filled the air as Lander screamed in pain. His head had landed first, hitting some of the Legos that were lying on the floor. Blood gushed from the back of his head as he screamed in pain.

John picked Lander up and frantically looked around for something to stop the bleeding. Grabbing a clean diaper, he pressed it against the head wound with even pressure. He glanced at the woman who just sat there staring ahead. Bridget's arms, the arms that had not reached to stop her son's fall, now lay empty on her lap. She never reached out to comfort her son. Without thinking and with no emotion, John pulled back and slapped Bridget hard across the face. The sound of the slap startled John for a second, as if someone else had done it. For a split second he paused, but turning away from the woman who ignored him, he ran down the stairs with Lander moaning in his arms.

"Call 911," John shouted as rushed downstairs.

Regina ran out of her study and seeing Lander bleeding in her son-in-law's arms she answered, "There's no time. I'll drive you to the hospital."

Hannah opened the door of her room, and ran to join them.

"No!" shouted John. "I left Lowell alone with his mother!"

Hannah paused, and then turned to attend to the younger twin.

John trembled, holding his limp son while Regina broke every speed limit. Arriving at the same hospital where Lander was born, John rushed his son into the E.R., past the front desk and into the back. Regina followed quickly after giving information to the nurse and found Lander already being examined by the E.R. physician. Lander was rushed up to C.A.T. scan, as both John and Regina waited for news.

It seemed like a lifetime but the results of the test arrived with Lander's return.

"I have good news," the muscular doctor announced. "It is just a deep laceration. There is no skull fracture and we can't see any permanent damage."

"But he hit the floor so hard!" John responded.

"Kids are a lot tougher than we realize. Head wounds bleed a lot and cause a lot of scare, but we're lucky. With a few stitches he should be fine. We'll keep him overnight for observation, just to make sure. He should be able to go home tomorrow morning," answered the doctor as he prepared to stitch the wound.

"I'll stay with him tonight," John whispered in relief. "Regina, you go home and check on Lowell. He must be so frightened!"

Regina's face filled with anger and disdain. "I'm not leaving Lander tonight. It's your fault this happened! You should have been more careful!"

John again felt the impulse to slap someone across the face, but this time he resisted, "All right, we both can stay. Just let me call Hannah to let her know that Lander is all right and to check on Lowell."

Hannah returned to Bridget's room after answering the phone call from Mr. Laverty. The room was so eerily silent.

Lowell had watched silently as his father ran from the room with Lander in his arms. Looking up he saw the single tear that escaped his mother's eye and cascaded down her reddened cheek. Crawling across the floor, the small boy wrapped his arms around his mother's leg and clung to her. That is how Hannah found him and that is how he remained.

Consider it all joy, my brothers, when you encounter various trials, for you know that the testing of your faith produces perseverance. And let that perseverance be perfect, so that you may be perfect and complete, lacking in nothing.
—*James1:2–3*

Chapter Three

A blessed child may be born to a smiling mother of plenty, another to a tearful mother who doesn't know how she will find the money to feed another mouth. Some babies are welcomed with pride, wanted by fathers, grandparents, and neighbors. Others are born into shame—hidden by young, unmarried girls, born of rape, incest, or just a momentary need to be loved. Some newborns are laid in fluffy cribs in nurseries of their own, while some are found crying in dumpsters hidden in dark alleys. Only one thing is sure with each birth: God created and loves each child. Each child is wanted, born with a purpose known only to God.

Skylar was born with blond downy hair and large brown eyes that looked into the eyes of a mother who loved her. No one else came to the hospital. The father, who had denied his paternity, was attending a college lecture in another state. Her grandparents, who had advised their daughter to get an abortion, refused to support her "bad" decision. Her friends had all turned away in shame. Only one man came. John had driven Hannah to the hospital.

Just weeks before, while John gave Hannah a ride to her final appointment with the obstetrician, he seemed to sense how alone she was.

"Do you have anyone to be with you when the time comes?" he asked.

Hannah was ashamed. None of her family was speaking to her. They had let her know in no uncertain terms that she had brought disgrace on the family. She had hoped that they would soften as the birth of their first grandchild got closer but her latest attempt to reach out to her mother had been spurned.

"No, no one seems to be interested in this baby. My family doesn't want anything to do with me." she responded.

"How about the father? Do you hear from him?" John asked.

Hannah could feel her eyes stink with the tears she tried to hold back, "No, he seems less interested than my family."

After an awkward moment of silence, John spoke up, "I wonder if you would mind if I stayed with you during the birth. I think the miracle of birth is one of the great moments in life."

Hannah wanted to shout with joy. Someone finally seemed to care. Instead, she whispered softly, trying to maintain her composure, "I would be happy for you to come with me."

"Breathe…" he advised as he puffed in sympathy. Allowed into the delivery room by the mistaken belief of the nurses that he was the father, John stood at the head of the stretcher trying to remember the breathing techniques he had learned before the twins were born. Hannah lay sweaty, with hair matted. She bit her lip during the waves of pain that heralded life. This birth was easier, and much more routine, than Bridget's. John couldn't help but compare the only two births he had ever attended and despite his faith he questioned God about the difference. When Skylar was born and placed in Hannah's welcoming arms, a momentary thought of the wife who didn't reach out to her own children entered his memory. John shook the thought from his mind. He had no right to compare the two women. He was married.

He stayed that evening, making sure that Hannah and Skylar

were doing well. Returning home, he found himself explaining the birth of the nanny's baby girl to a non-responsive Bridget. He had hoped that the news of another birth might stir the maternal instinct of his wife. However, there was no reaction. Sighing, he rose and left for another night in an empty bed. Checking on the boys, he found them fast asleep in their shared bedroom. They had been so excited about the new baby when he and Hannah left for the hospital. It had been many hours since they had left and it was long past the boys' bedtime. *They're even different in the way they sleep,* laughed John. Lander lay sprawled across his twin bed, arms and legs hanging off the edge. Lowell was wrapped in his blankets. A tiny bundle in the middle of his bed, as if cocooned for protection, he was hard to see.

John hadn't realized how exhausted he was until he was walking down the hall to his bedroom. When he heard his mother-in-law's bedroom door open, he cringed.

"Is it over?" Regina demanded as he tried to hurry past.

"Yes, she had a beautiful baby girl. She named her Skylar."

"Humph! What kind of a name is that?" Regina asked with disdain.

"Hannah says it was one of the names on her short list. She decided on the name Skylar when she noticed how cloudlessly blue the sky was as we rode to the hospital."

"That's the stupidest thing I have ever heard! What is the last name of the baby going to be? She isn't married, after all!" snorted Regina.

John could feel his face redden.

"Well, at least we can start looking for a more suitable nanny!" pronounced Regina.

John sighed. His hands shook as he looked down at his feet, "Hannah needs time to recoup. She can continue to care for the twins while adjusting to taking care of little Skylar," John said.

Regina slammed her door in anger. *I'm sick of him telling me what is best for my grandson,* she thought. *I'll get rid of that girl yet!*

*

Hannah was shocked when she opened the door to her room. Inside was a wicker bassinet covered with pink bows. A changing table, loaded with lotions and diapers, stood in the corner. John, who had picked Hannah up at the hospital, followed behind with her bag.

"I hope you like everything. I had a friend of Bridget's buy what she thought a new baby girl would need."

As Hannah opened the closet, she started to weep. A pole had been added to the bottom half and on that pole hung dozens of pink newborn outfits.

"Oh my goodness, what a wonderful gift! How can I ever thank you, Mr. Laverty?"

"You can start by calling me John," he answered as he placed her suitcase by the door. "And once you are settled, bring Skylar to see Bridget. I think that seeing a baby may just get her interest."

"I'll be happy to," Hannah replied as she laid Skylar in her new bassinet. "As soon as I get her dressed up, I'll visit Bridget and let her see the baby."

Turning, she felt her heart catch as he grinned while quietly shutting the door. His blue eyes sparkled, enjoying her pleasure at the new baby things. As he closed the door to her new bedroom, she shook her head dismissing the momentary feeling. *I never noticed how handsome he is,* she thought as she turned to change the baby. Pushing the thought of him from her mind, Hannah changed the infant.

Hannah didn't notice that she was smiling to herself as she dressed the baby in one of the filly pretty dresses from the closet and placed a pink bow in Skylar's soft hair. Little pink booties completed the look. She sat beside Bridget and talked to the non-responsive woman about the birth and her newborn. For just a flicker of a moment, Hannah thought she saw a look of interest on Bridget's face but the emotion disappeared so quickly that she couldn't be sure. Within a few minutes, the twins came bouncing in, excited to see the new baby themselves.

Lander ran quickly to Hannah with a look of delight, stopping just short of crashing into her.

"Whoa there, Lander," John called as he entered the room behind the two boys. "You have to be careful with a new baby. Be gentle, now!"

Lander smiled in delight as the baby squirmed around, and opened her eyes.

"She's looking at me!" Lander shouted in delight.

"Yes," answered Hannah, "Skylar seems to like you."

"Skylar! That's her name?" asked the two-year-old.

Hannah just smiled as she held the baby closer to the young boy. Lowell hung back, as if confused by the new baby, his eyes wide and staring.

"Go on, Lowell," encouraged John. "The baby won't hurt you."

Lowell slowly crept up to the baby that Lander had already lost interest in. As he fearfully reached out to touch her, Skylar wrapped her fingers around his larger finger. Lowell smiled as Skylar opened her eyes and gurgled.

"She really likes you!" Hannah announced, as Skylar gripped tighter.

Lowell stood transfixed. He couldn't seem to pull himself away. It wasn't until John started talking to Bridget that he retreated to his familiar corner. However, a slight grin never left his face.

Hannah listened to the gentleness of John's voice as he talked to his wife. Although she continued to stare out the window, John spoke to her as if they were carrying on a two-way conversation. First, he talked about the baby. Then he shared the latest from his job. Hannah's heart ached for the man who seemed to be talking to himself.

I could make him happy—the thought that quickened her mind startled her. *What am I thinking? He's a married man and my boss!*

Confused by her own musings, Hannah rose to leave. "I better let the baby rest."

"You should get some rest yourself. Don't worry, I've hired a temporary nurse to watch the boys for the next three weeks. She can also watch over Skylar whenever you need a rest." replied John as he turned to Bridget.

Hannah did go to bed, after comfortably placing Skylar in cotton pajamas in her new bassinet. She was more exhausted than she realized.

The dreams that rippled through her sleep were visions of John and her together. They were married and raising the three children as if they were their own. She saw herself laughing and kissing him. In her dream, there was no Bridget, only her and John. She ran her fingers lovingly through his thick black hair, and looked into his sparkling blue eyes. He came closer and held her to him.

That is when Hannah woke in a sweat. Looking around, she realized that it was all just a dream. *A dream that will never come true,* she thought. After checking on the baby, she settled down, but tossed and turned with worry over her emotions. *I have to go to someone, these feelings aren't right,* she thought. Despite her emotions, exhausted by childbirth, she fell asleep.

Night after night the dreams recurred. Despite her prayers and intentions, she couldn't seem to stop them. Just a week later Hannah took the afternoon off. Leaving the baby in the care of the nurse, she took the bus downtown. Only three elderly people stood in line and Hannah waited.

When it was her turn, she entered the confessional and knelt.

"Bless me Father for I have sinned. It has been a month since my last confession."

She hesitated, not knowing how to word her concern.

"What is it, my child?"

"I have sinned in my thoughts and in my desires. I think I may be falling in love with my boss, a married man."

The priest, hidden behind the screen, asked some questions, to gain understanding of Hannah's circumstances.

She started to quietly sob. His probing words highlighted the feeling she tried to submerge.

"My child, you have not sinned but you are under great temptation to do so."

"But what can I do? I need my job. And I love the children I care for!"

The priest's soft voice was comforting, "You need to find another place to live. Living down the hall from a man you find attractive is asking for trouble. Isn't there another place for you and your child?"

"The grandmother wanted me to stay in the small carriage house on the property. She didn't like me living on the same floor as the family. My boss, though, wanted me close to the twins when they were newborns," Hannah whispered.

"Well, now you must make the change. The need to be alone with your baby is a legitimate reason. The change will help you deal with the temptation," the priest instructed.

"But I have prayed. The feelings just seem to grow stronger," she answered.

"How have you prayed, my child?"

"I have asked God to remove the temptation. I have vowed to force my thoughts away from John," Hannah sobbed.

"I want you to try a different prayer. I want you to pray for his wife. I want you to say a rosary each day for her recovery and the healing of their marriage. Could you do that each day?" the priest asked.

"Why yes, I love the rosary."

"I believe you'll learn to only want the best for the wife. It's been my experience that you can't harm someone you are praying for," the priest advised.

Hannah left the confessional after routine prayers and penance. Her head was spinning. Would all these changes make her love John less? Somehow she doubted it.

Jesus answered him, "If anyone loves me, he will keep my word, and my Father will love him, and we will come to him and make our home with him.
—*John 14:23*

Chapter Four

The homes we live in are not ours. We are visitors, tourists. Our true home is not of this world and the homes we love and know on this earth are whispers, ghosts. Earthly homes, no matter how much we love them or how attached we are to them, are a mere foreshadowing of the eternal home that awaits us.

Hannah made the move to the carriage house during a weekday. She didn't want to have John around. She got the caretaker and gardener to help her knowing that John would be busy teaching school. It was strange; she just didn't want the image of him in her new home. She was finding it hard enough to wipe the thought of him from her mind. Each night, when her inhibitions were relaxed by sleep, the dreams would come. Wave after wave, the visions would continue all through the night. Often she was glad to be awoken by the baby. Skylar's cries ended the visions of a love that could never be. Moving to the carriage house was quick and easy. Hannah had so little to bring over, just her clothing. Most of the things carried by the caretaker and gardener were the beautiful gifts given to the baby. The carriage house was fully furnished and functional. It had been used as a guest house in the early years when the Kagans gave gala parties. When Regina's husband was still alive, they had been known for their seasonal gatherings. The men would dress in tuxedoes and the women in designer gowns. The Kagans would greet the guests as if they were holding court. If any of the guests had traveled or just had a little too much champagne they would stay in the carriage house.

The tiny house had two bedrooms, a small sitting room, a tiny but quaint kitchen, and a functional bath. The loveliest thing about the small fieldstone home was the hedged English-style garden that graced the back. It was completely private. It was surrounded by evergreen hedges that the gardener kept trimmed at seven feet, and the only outward entry was a swinging garden gate on the side of the drive. The other entry was through the kitchen door that led to a small deck with steps to the enclosed backyard. Within the hedges were raised gardens of different dimensions that contained either flowers or vegetables. Between the raised platforms were mulched walking paths and the corners of the hedges held rose bushes and fruit trees. Across from the garden gate were ornate wrought-iron chairs and tables. Looking out from the chair, the visitor could see the brightly painted bird houses that were home to Northern blue birds and a family of cardinals who enjoyed splashing around the cement bird bath below. Hannah was in love with the garden, which was maintained by the family gardener.

*

Regina had been happy to send her men to move the nanny. *One step away, and one step out,* she mused with glee as she watched Hannah move. She wanted the woman gone and felt her patience was wearing thin.

Hannah lived in the carriage house for a year and during that year there had been a marked improvement in Bridget's condition. She was now not confining herself to her childhood room. It shocked all of them when Bridget walked down the stairs to the breakfast table. Silently she ate her breakfast with Regina and John. And while she never talked and remained distracted, it was a miracle that filled John with joy. Each day, Bridget walked around the house, seemingly with purpose and intent. She ate her meals in the dining room with her mother and husband each day, and after being dressed by the nurse, could be found in any room, any room but the bedroom she slept in.

Hannah spent most of her days with the boys and Skylar in the boy's play room upstairs. The first time that Bridget entered the room it shocked everyone. Within a week, it became common for Bridget to spend most of the day sitting in the corner rocking chair. She never interacted with the children or Hannah. She never responded to the children. Occasionally, a slight smile would grace her, as if she were amused by something. Lander soon ignored her as Hannah played with the boys and taught them their colors and numbers. Lowell sat close to his mother, often at her feet. As the boys quickly passed through toddlerhood, Lowell was often found talking to Bridget. She seemed to watch his every move.

In the late afternoon, Hannah took Skylar and went home to the cottage. She tried to leave before John got home from school. *Better to see him as little as possible,* she thought as she did her best to avoid him. She would often run into him on the weekends when he visited the boys at play, but things seemed easier now that Bridget was often present in the playroom. It helped to watch John interacting with his wife and children. It reminded Hannah of her place in his life.

Warm summer evenings were spent in the garden with Skylar. The mother and daughter relished the privacy of the yard, watching the flowers that bloomed and the daughter who was learning to walk filled Hannah with a sense of purpose. On the nights she had school, she would bring Skylar to the child-care facility that the community college provided. Most evenings she would study and read as Skylar explored the garden around her. Life seemed to settle into a pleasant routine. Hannah had changed her plans. A four- year teaching degree would take too long, and she didn't trust herself to be around John without reaching out to him. She had decided to study for a nursing degree. *Just two years to independence and a good paycheck to support Skylar,* she mused, as she struggled to memorize the skeletal system. She was deep in the middle of her anatomy chapter, when she heard the garden gate being unlatched.

Looking up, she was shocked to see John. He stood with a wide grin, watching Skylar pulling at a marigold which clung to the roots that anchored it to the ground. She almost fell backwards as her newly acquired balance was not yet strong. The tow-haired toddler was soon enough distracted by a butterfly that winged its way by. Still wearing the amused grin, John looked up and waved to Hannah. She didn't want to see him, here in her garden, but her heart leapt as his eyes sparkled.

"Hi there, I'm sorry to disturb you while you're studying. I needed to talk to you about this coming fall, and I rarely seem to see you anymore," John said.

Hannah swallowed hard, so taken with his rough good looks. "Don't worry, I needed a break anyway," she smiled weakly, as he sat in the chair beside her. "What is it that you want to discuss?"

"I signed the boys up for a year of nursery school. They'll be going for half days three days a week. It's hard to believe but they will be going full-time to kindergarten next year and this will help prepare them for the change," John nodded.

"Are you trying to tell me that you won't have a need for a full-time nanny anymore?" Hannah looked away and reddened.

John's eyes opened wide. "Oh no! Nothing like that! I just wanted to talk to you about the schedule and ask if you would have a problem getting them to the bus and picking them up when school is over. The bus will be picking the boys up and dropping them off at the end of the drive, just outside your gate. I don't know if you set your schedule for school yet and wanted to let you know."

Hannah sighed with relief. She had another year until she could earn her diploma and didn't want to look for a new job yet. *Besides, I love my little home almost as much as I love this man.* She shook her head in an attempt to shake the thoughts from her mind.

"No, I think it will be a great thing for the boys to learn to mix with other children. I can spend a little more time with Skylar. She is growing so fast. Soon she will be off to kindergarten herself," answered Hannah, not looking toward John.

As if on cue, Skylar with her blond curls bouncing in the sunlight ran up the deck step and reached her chubby arms out toward John. "Daddy, Daddy!" she cried indicating she wanted to be picked up by the visitor.

Hannah could feel the sweat forming on her brow. "Oh, I'm so sorry! That's the first time she ever used that word! I'm so sorry!"

John laughed as he picked Skylar up and swung her up in the air. "It's okay, I'm the only man she ever sees so it's a natural assumption on her part."

"I'll try to explain it to her, but I don't know how much she will understand at her age." Hannah could feel her body tremble. *I wish you were her father!* She thought as he swung Skylar, full of giggles, through the air.

She watched as he took his leave. The garden, so full of late summer blossoms and vegetables about to be harvested seemed empty when he closed the garden gate behind him. Hannah could feel the tears welling up in her eyes. This was exactly what she didn't want. She had hoped to never have the image of John in her little cottage, or even the cottage garden. It had been a world apart, a safe haven. Safe from the unrealistic dream of having this man in her life, and Hannah knew that the dream of John smiling by the gate and lifting her daughter up in the air would permeate her every imagining. Her dreams would now be invaded by the unrequited and forbidden love that grew ever deeper in her heart. Still, she had to control her feelings. She had to finish school before she could leave this temptation behind.

Hannah pulled out her Rosary beads and prayed. She prayed for the wife who stood between herself and her heart's desire. *Oh, how I wish that John was Skylar's father,* she thought as she lost herself in the 'Hail Mary.'

*

The Japanese maple's leaves blazed a deepened red as September cooled the world with northern breezes. The alarm blared after Hannah was already in the shower and coffee was brewing in the tiny kitchen. It woke little Skylar who, in padded pajama feet, wandered from her bed bleary-eyed. It was much earlier than she was used to and she had no way of knowing that this new early awakening was to become a habit for three days a week. Hannah was prepared to get Lander and Lowell ready for their first day of nursery school. She wrapped her damp and freshly shampooed hair up in a twisted bun, and threw on her jeans. Rushing, she quickly dressed Skylar and headed toward the main house. The twins had trouble getting up as Hannah washed and dressed them in their new clothes. Lander seemed excited, talking non-stop about all the new friends he planned to make at school. Lowell stood pale and silent. His lip started to quiver as the four walked down the drive to meet the scheduled bus. Hannah held Skylar's hand as the boys walked ahead of her. Lander rushed, anxious to get to school with his new classmates, while Lowell silently dragged his feet.

The yellow bus stopped at the end of the driveway. Lander jumped up the metal steps and with a wide grin ran to an open seat. Lowell pulled back as his little body shook with fear.

Squatting down, Hannah took both of his shoulders and whispered calmly, "You'll like school. Don't be afraid. This afternoon you can tell me all about the new friends you made."

Lowell with his pointer finger in his mouth looked doubtfully at the bus. With a deep sigh, he slowly made his way up the steps with an air of resignation. He slid alone into the first empty bench seat, looking sadly out the window at Hannah.

Poor little thing, she thought as the bus pulled away. Letting go of Skylar's hand, Hannah waved good-bye to the tiny figure. Suddenly, a bright blue butterfly flew by. Skylar took off chasing the butterfly into the street. Hannah screamed, and reached out, but Skylar was too fast for her. As the opposing traffic that had been stopped by the red lights of the school bus started up again the lead car gunned his gas, apparently late for his day at work. Hannah ran out into the street just as the driver, seeing Skylar, slammed on his brakes.

The sound of the screeching brakes and the smell of the burning rubber was the last thing Hannah heard. Pushing Skylar, who now stood frozen in fear, Hannah managed to thrust her safely to the opposite curb. Saving her daughter, she couldn't save herself.

Hannah's body lay sprawled over the hood of the car that hit her full force. Skylar cried without understanding that the mother who just saved her life couldn't answer her call.

"Whoever will not receive you or listen to your words—go outside that house or town and shake the dust from your feet"
—Matthew 10: 14

Chapter Five

Moments define us. It is the simple choices that will determine what friends we make, the town we live in, or even the partner we marry. Like adventurers we plunge ahead unaware of the magnitude of our decisions. Perhaps it is in these decisions we are guided by forces unseen. We think that we have made the logical decision based on facts when we are actually led by spiritual forces beyond our understanding.

When John heard the sirens, he was putting on his jacket and getting ready for another day in the classroom. Looking out the upstairs window, he could see the swirling lights of numerous police cars at the end of the drive. *Jesus, don't let it be the boys!* his mind screamed. John felt as if his heart would pound right out of his chest. Running down the stairs, he ignored the enquiry of his mother-in-law who had been aroused from bed by the noise. Sprinting down the long drive, he broke into a sweat because of the huge crowd that blocked his vision. *Where are the twins?* his mind cried as he finally reached the end of the drive. He could see a female police officer holding Skylar in her arms and headed right to her.

"What's happening? Where are my sons?" he asked in a panic, as the officer turned to face him.

Skylar reached out to be held by John, as the young officer held her tighter. "Are you the girl's father?"

"No, No! Her mother is my nanny. Where is Hannah? Where are my sons?" he shouted.

Another officer approached. "Was the nanny waiting for the school bus with your boys?"

"Yes!" shouted John, with his heart pounding.

"Don't worry. The accident happened after the bus pulled out. I'm sure your boys are safe and at school already," the male officer reassured him.

John blanched. He couldn't take this strange policeman's word for it. With his hands sweating and his vision blurred by the perspiration pouring off his forehead he dialed his cell and desperately waited for the school office to pick up.

"Hello—hello! This is John Laverty. There's been a terrible accident and I need to be sure that my boys made it to school all right," he cried to the secretary on the other end of the line.

"Give me a minute and I'll check," she responded, putting him on hold.

It was the longest minute of his life.

Returning, she comforted him, "they are both here-safe and sound."

He let out a long sigh of relief, not aware that he had been holding his breath—both Lander and Lowell were safe in their new classroom.

Turning, John asked, "What's happened? Where is Hannah?"

The older officer grimaced. "Is Hannah the name of the nanny?"

He paused while John nodded in the affirmative. "I'm afraid she didn't fare as well. The witnesses tell us that the nanny pushed the baby girl out of harm's way, only to get hit herself. She saved the baby who had apparently run into the street. The driver had no way of seeing the girl as she ran from behind the bus," he said.

"Where is Hannah? Was she hurt? Can I see her?" John answered rapid fire.

The mature officer glanced knowingly at the female officer who was holding Skylar. "I'm sorry but she was just pronounced dead. Can you give me her full name and address? We will have to notify the family."

Hannah's dead? John's mind couldn't comprehend it, but he physically reached for little Skylar.

"Is she your daughter?" repeated the female officer, as she clung to the toddler.

"She's the nanny's daughter," answered John in a pained whisper.

"We'll need the family information for the mother. Until then the girl will be placed with Child Protective Services. Do you have that information?"

"I'll have to go back to my home office and check the file I have on Hannah. I never met her family," John said, feeling numb he headed up the drive with the grey-haired policeman.

Looking back, he watched as the E.M.T.'s arrived for Hannah's body. Skylar cried as she watched him leave, reaching out her chubby arms for him to take her. It all seemed surreal and John kept hoping to wake up and find it was all a nightmare.

Regina Kagan, dressed in a silk robe, fired questions at them as soon as they entered the foyer.

"Is Lander all right? Where is he?" John was grateful when the officer took it upon himself to quiet her fears.

"Is Lander one of your grandsons? If so, he is safely at school," he answered. As he walked toward his office, John noticed Bridget sitting quietly in a side chair in the foyer. He squatted before her and took both of her shoulders in his hands. "Bridget, the boys and the baby are all right. There's been an accident, a terrible accident, but all of the children are safe and sound."

There was no response but he thought he saw a glimmer of joy in her eyes. *Perhaps, it's just wishful thinking on my part*, he thought. John retrieved Hannah's file. It had all the information that the officer needed.

"As Hannah's employer, I think I should be the one to inform her family. Can I do that?" John asked.

"Yes, but I will drive you over. Sometimes in circumstances like these the reaction can be overwhelming," answered the officer. "I've dealt with this kind of thing more than once but it never gets easier."

John's head was spinning. "Do you think we should bring the boys home?"

Regina grabbed her chance at control. "Why do that? The twins are better off where they are. I'll be here when they get home."

John, thinking of telling Hannah's family, just nodded agreement as he followed the officer out the door.

Knocking on the front door of the small Cape Cod home, he was shocked when a young man answered. Tall, dark, and thin he turned out to be Hannah's younger brother.

He's the spitting image of Hannah, thought John as he was invited into the small living room. Hannah's brother had the same grey eyes. It unnerved John.

A tiny woman with a short white bob sat on a worn couch in the living room. She seemed upset to have her world disturbed as she picked up the remote and muted the game show she had been watching. A balding man, who identified himself as Hannah's father, walked out of the back kitchen and stood in the doorway. He seemed a little more curious than the woman.

Introducing himself as Hannah's boss, John began, "I don't know how to tell you this. It's about Hannah. She…"

The pause extended as John groped for the right words.

The policeman took over. "I am sorry that we are here with such terrible news," he started, knowing it was best to prepare them for the worst. "Your daughter Hannah has been in a car accident. I'm afraid she didn't make it. She died saving your granddaughter. The baby is fine. Not a scratch on her. You should be proud of your daughter—she gave her life to save another."

The brother's face blanched with shock. As the tears started to well up in his eyes, he turned and pounded the wall with his fist. "No, not Hannah. She can't be dead!"

John watched the mother who continued to sit. She just stared straight ahead as they gave her the news of her daughter's death. The woman appeared to be frozen. *She's in shock*, thought John.

Turning, he was stunned to see the father take another sip of his coffee, as if he had just been told that the mail was delivered. His face betrayed no feeling. John felt a shiver run down his spine. Perhaps they didn't comprehend.

The officer continued, "It's a blessing that your granddaughter is fine. I know she can't replace your daughter, but raising her will be a comfort to you."

John watched as the mother finally stirred. "I have no granddaughter. My daughter is dead and I want nothing to do with the evidence of her sin."

Shocked, John spoke out. "You can't mean that. Skylar is a beautiful child, a gift from God."

The father answered, "Whatever that child is has nothing to do with God. She was born outside of God's will and we want nothing to do with her."

Hannah's brother turned in anger. "How can you say that? She's your granddaughter and my niece."

Turning to John, the brother continued, "If they don't want her I'll raise her."

"Not if you want to go to college. I won't pay your tuition if you defy us. Besides, you're just seventeen and no court in the land would give you custody. I won't see your life destroyed by your sister's mistake!" shouted the father.

John was stunned as the boy bowed his head in submission. He could feel his temper rising. "You don't understand. Hannah gave her life to save Skylar. She watched her mother get hit by the car. She will need all the love you can give her."

The father's face hardened as he turned his attention to the police officer. "There's no law that says we have to take the child, is there?"

"No. There's no law that forces you to take her!" he answered coldly.

"Then we don't want her," spoke the woman on the couch. "She is nothing to us."

"Don't you want to see her before you make that decision?" begged John.

"No need to," answered Hannah's father. "Our mind is made up."

John's eyes opened with shock. He couldn't believe his ears. It seemed that Hannah's actions had made her dead to them already. And Skylar, the visible evidence of her sin, wasn't welcome in their home. It sickened him.

The policeman rose and sighed, "Well, you've been notified. You can claim your daughter's body at the morgue to make funeral arrangements"

"We have no daughter," answered the mother as John shook his head in disgust. When the door was closed behind him, John paused in total disbelief.

Turning to the officer, he shook his head. "I can't believe them. They don't even want to bury their only daughter!"

"I've seen this before. Perhaps they'll come around. If not, the city will bury her in Potter's field," he responded.

John could feel the anger rising as the police car turned toward home. "And they don't want the baby. What will happen to her?"

"She'll be placed in a foster home. Someone will come along and adopt her. She's a pretty little thing," answered the policeman, trying to reassure John.

"No stranger is going to take Skylar, and Hannah is not going to be buried in an unmarked grave. Where do I go to adopt her?" John asked.

The officer smiled. *She'll be okay now. Her mother didn't die in vain!* he thought as he changed direction. *I'll take this man right over.*

John, full of determination, didn't even question why they drove to the office of Social Services instead of straight home. A thin woman with large glasses greeted them. Explaining the situation, both John and the policeman watched as she checked her computer to find Skylar in the system.

"Yes," here she is. We are looking for a temporary foster home to place her for the night."

John was quick to answer, "I want to adopt her. Can't I take her home tonight? She's been through so much and it would be better for her to be with people she knows and who love her."

Looking over her glasses, the woman paused, and then responded.

"To tell you the truth, Mr. Laverty, it will take a long time to get approved for adoption. If I may make a suggestion I think you should apply to foster little Skylar. If you get your approval she could be home with your family by late tonight."

John quickly filled out the papers to become a foster father. After a background check he was approved and assured that Skylar would be home by late that evening.

"When things settle down I'll start adoption procedures." He announced as the officer drove him home. John was determined to give Skylar a home.

"Behold, I tell you a mystery. We shall not all fall asleep, but we will all be changed, in an instant, in the blink of an eye, at the last trumpet. For the trumpet will sound, the dead will be raised incorruptible, and we shall be changed."
—*1Corinthians 15: 51*

Chapter Six

Death snatches them away, before their time, before we can say goodbye, before we are ready to let them go. One day, they are sitting among us and the next they are gone. Our hearts ache as we turn, expecting them to open the door and smile. We reach for the phone to share a joke or a piece of news and remember that they are not there to answer.

We go to places that we shared with them and all we can see is the ghost of our friend. And each time it happens we remember that they will never return. To reach them we must wait, wait until it is our time to leave. So we continue our journey, a little lonely, a little empty, hoping to be reunited with those who have gone before us. And in their leaving we find the grave that awaits us a little less fearsome and a little less cold.

It was a small funeral, Hannah's. Yet so many more came then were expected. Of course, Regina Kagan came, more for appearance then for caring. She wore a black dress with pearls and a large brim hat. Dark glasses completed the look and were more to hide the fact that she had no tears than to cover grief up. She watched from the pew as her daughter and son-in-law entered with the twins dressed in little suits and ties. Their black shoes shone with polish and the cleats on them tapped all the way down the aisle of the church. John held Skylar, who was confused and unaware of the gravity of her situation, in his arms.

Nannies who worked in the area trickled in, dressed in their best to honor one of their own. It surprised Regina to learn that Hannah was so loved, having filled in for others during emergencies and for advising the inexperienced with sage advice. The media came. It was a feel-good story to run in the Sunday paper—"Nanny gives life to save a child, Mother saves her own." The story continued as front page news for another two days until a political scandal took its place.

Regina Kagan watched for Hannah's family. She had a plan to convince them to take Skylar and raise her as their own. *Even if it costs me a pretty penny, I need to remove that child from the nursery,* she thought. She was prepared to offer a monthly payment to rid her home of the unwanted brat. Disappointed, she realized that no one from Hannah's family came. Even in death the shame of an unwed mother closed their hearts.

As if to give lie to the pain of the situation, the church glowed. The alabaster statues of the Blessed Mother and St. Joseph stood on either side of the ornate white marble altar. The life-size crucifix hung on the wall behind the altar and became the center of the church as was the golden tabernacle beneath it. The side walls were covered with stained glass windows that, while letting in the morning sun, depicted the passion of Christ.

Slowly the coffin was carried up the center aisle. The grieving congregation turned when Hannah was placed beneath the altar of God. As the Father Logan sprinkled the casket with holy water, the voices of the congregation rose in undulating song, "He will raise you up on angel's wings, bear you on the breath of dawn. Make you to rise like sun, and hold you—hold you in the palm of His Hand."

Skylar squirmed on John's lap and placed her arms around Bridget's neck. She seemed to want a woman to hold her. John watched his wife as she reached up and held the girl closely. Bridget was starting to respond to others. It had been four years, numerous doctors, and many prayers, but she was slowly coming back. *Perhaps Skylar would be good for her—a little girl!* Thought John, as the Mass continued. The little blond laid her head on Bridget's shoulder and found a semblance of comfort.

Father Logan spoke softly of sacrifice and the purest reflection of love. Jesus gave his life for us as an example of perfect love and Hannah followed His example. Regina shook her head in disbelief as some of the women in the pew behind her openly wept for the loss of their friend and fellow nanny.

After Mass each of the attendees walked around the coffin that was draped with the white cloth that represented Hannah's Christian life and Baptism. Given a red carnation, each person placed the flower on the wood coffin. John had seen to it that Hannah had the best. She was to be laid to rest in the Catholic cemetery just a mile away. *Some day Skylar will be able to visit the grave of the mother who died for her,* he thought as they headed for the cemetery. He was still in shock over Hannah's family's cold reaction to her death. They never called to check on Skylar. They didn't come to the wake or funeral. *I'll raise Skylar myself,* he thought.

The day seemed endless. Food was catered at the mansion to feed all of those who knew and loved Hannah. Everyone seemed to have a story about how she had helped them. Her kindness had touched everyone who knew her. *I never really knew her,* John thought. *I knew how wonderful she was with the children, but I never knew how very special she was to everyone.* No one seemed to want to leave. It was as if in leaving they would have to put their memories away. As if times of kindness and love could be folded and put away in a drawer. Life would intrude and Hannah would be forgotten. It was late when the last guest finally left. John was drained. All through the services, he had suppressed his grief. His pain grew deeper with every tale of how special Hannah had been. He just wanted to collapse into his bed. But Regina wasn't about to let him.

Regina chose this moment to attack his decision to raise Skylar. Regina was irate about keeping the girl. Since Hannah's death she had been like a spider watching from her web. Now she saw her chance and pounced. As John and Bridget sat in the parlor, she started.

"She is not welcome here!" Regina shouted as John turned away from her.

"She would be better off being adopted by a family of her own," she continued to rant, as her son-in-law ignored her.

The children had been put to sleep upstairs. John was exhausted, both physically and emotionally. *Not now!* his mind screamed as he sat there. He held his head in both hands.

Regina knew when her enemy was weak. She knew it was the best time to attack.

No! I won't have that whore's child raised with my grandson! she thought. Regina was determined to win this argument. John wouldn't look at her. With his jaw clamped, he just continued to stare at the floor.

"I refuse to allow that child to stay here in my home. She doesn't belong here. Personally, I think you're being selfish. Child Services can find her a home of her own, a home with people who want her," Regina continued.

John looked up. "I want her. She is part of this family."

"Don't you ever think about your own family? Is it right to split your limited time between Lander and this strange girl? It's like you don't care about the time she would steal away from him," continued Regina. She paced up and down the length of the parlor, so full of energy she couldn't contain herself.

John noticed that she never mentioned Lowell. "I think it would be good for the boys to have a little sister. She belongs here and here is where she is staying."

Regina stopped and stood over John as if to emphasize her point. "What about my daughter? What about her feelings? Do you think she wants some other woman's child as part of her family? Bridget is just starting to get well. Don't you care about her? This could set her recovery back by years. Don't you care about my daughter?"

John couldn't believe his ears, and he knew the power this woman held. He wouldn't put it past her to contact one of her political friends and have Skylar taken away. He would have to stand up to her, but he could feel his heart fluttering, his stomach cramping. However, the thought of Hannah giving her life to save the girl gave him a shot of courage. "I am going to adopt Skylar and there is nothing you can do about it."

A cold smile spread across Regina's face. John had seen that look before. "Oh!" she answered in a whisper that was more frightening than her shouting, "there's nothing I can do, is there?"

She let the statement lie—heavy upon the stale air of the stuffy living room. Silence like a damp blanket covered the three of them as the truth of what Regina was capable of was realized.

John felt light-headed. He was not used to arguing with this kind of power. He was practiced in the art of avoidance. *I can't avoid this*, he thought as he looked up to see the smug look on Regina's face. Looking over at Bridget, who sat quietly with her hands folded on her lap, he knew that he stood alone. This woman was capable of anything, including destroying his career with one phone call. He had no doubt that she would use whatever power she possessed to win her way.

"I've made up my mind." John tried to sound firm, although his hands trembled. "I am adopting that little girl. If Bridget could talk, I am sure that she would agree with me. You can threaten all you want to—but I won't change my mind."

Regina's lip quivered with anger. "This is my house and that girl will not be staying here. Do you have any idea who you are talking to? That girl is not wanted and she will not be here by tomorrow!"

Pushing the terror he felt down, John rose to his feet. "You're right. This is your house and you have every right to put that child out."

Regina smiled, pleased that she had won. "I'm glad that you are finally seeing the truth. She doesn't belong here."

John stood poker straight. "If Skylar doesn't belong here then neither do we. If Skylar leaves then Bridget, myself, and the boys will all be going home together. Perhaps we have overstayed our welcome. Perhaps it is time for us to start living our own life."

Regina's face blanched. *I can't let him take Lander away!* Defeated by his threat, she stomped out of the room.

John collapsed back into the chair. The fight had taken all he had. His body quivered as the battle ended. It took him a few minutes to compose himself. As his heartbeat slowed, he heard Regina slamming doors in her frustration.

Looking up, he watched Bridget as she just sat still. She never moved, as if nothing had happened, as if she hadn't heard a word.

"Come on. It's late and I'm exhausted." He reached out and holding her arm guided his wife up the stairs.

After he left her with her nurse, John went to check on the boys. Lander was sprawled out in his bed and John covered his son with the blanket that was bunched up around his feet. Lowell lay in his flannel pajamas with his arm over Skylar who lay in the bed beside him. The sight made him smile. *She belongs here with us.*

Exhausted, John fell asleep as soon as his head hit the pillow. When he awoke the next morning, he vaguely remembered a small disturbance that roused him momentarily during the night. Looking over, he realized that it must have been when Bridget had crawled into bed beside him.

And in their greed they will exploit you with false words; from of old their condemnation has not been idle, and their destruction has not been asleep.
—*2 Peter 2:2–4*

Chapter Seven

In our dreams they come, like waves that grab the sand and then retreat. Memories are released from the hidden recesses of our mind, the mind that holds them captive during the day. At night, deep in dreams that set our memories free, our decisions all make sense. Awake, without understanding, we react to deep fears we don't understand. Ancient wisdom and nonsensical instincts direct us in superstitious ways.

Regina remembered the pain. She was meant to be tall like her mother but the malnutrition that caused rickets had weakened the bones in her legs. Her bones were stunted and so she became tiny. There was never enough food. Often there was no dinner at all. Her mother, tall and thin, would sigh.

"Now don't worry!" she would say, as she tucked the three siblings in the same bed, "Dad is sure to get that job down at the dock. One of his friends works there!" Of course, the promised job never came about. Still, Regina's mother never lost her smile.

"Regina, run down to the box and get the mail. Dad is sure to get that check. His family owes him money," her mother would cheerfully ask.

Regina learned to walk slowly down the path to the mailbox. In all the years they lived in the rented house on the edge of town, she never remembered receiving the promised check, the mystery check that was always on the way. Still, she never saw her mother give up hope. She spent all the years of Regina's childhood smiling. She ignored the constant smell of booze on her husband's breath, as he strolled home from the corner bar. Dressed in housecoats from the thrift store in town, she never questioned how he got the money for drinks but never had money for food.

As Regina grew she came to understand that her mother lived in a false world, a pretend world in which her husband loved the family and put them first. She ignored the truth. With eyes softened by illusion, she lived in a separate world in which happiness was always just around the corner. She never questioned her husband's actions. She never questioned her way of life. Her mother seemed to just float. She floated on the winds of chance—unable or unwilling to do anything to take control of her life.

Regina hated her father. She hated him for being an alcoholic and never finding anything but the occasional odd job. Her father was no good, but at least he never pretended to be worth anything. He never made promises that he didn't keep. He was what he was. He was the town drunk who kept his family in a drafty, heatless shack that most people wouldn't keep their dogs in. Regina grew up with the taunts of the other children in school. She patched up the worn dresses her mother supplied. She hid her shame behind an icy disdain for others. She took all her anger and poured it between the pages of her school books. Regina had the best marks in the school, determined to be the highest in something. She studied hard. It was easier to spend her evenings at the library. The library had heat. It was silent, not full of the false lies and stories of her mother. Regina may have hated her father, but she despised her mother the most.

Her brothers grew protective of the mother, blaming their father for their life of poverty. Regina blamed her mother. *Why does she lie to herself?* Regina wondered. It wasn't bad enough that she lived a lie. She dragged her children into the falsehood. And when she saw her two brothers feeding the illusions of her mother, she grew disgusted. *I will never let lies control me,* decided the watchful child. Regina became the guardian of the truth as she understood it—she became pragmatic.

She always did what was best for her, never letting emotions sway her. She liked the poor girl who lived across the street, but always made sure that she wasn't seen with her at school. At school, Regina walked past the girl as if she didn't know her. In school she joined all the clubs that placed her with the middle-class children. She didn't have any use for these children either. She considered them spoiled brats but she knew that they were of more use to her then the downtrodden children from her own neighborhood.

In high school she flirted with the football hero, winning him away from one of the most popular girls in town. Oh, there was plenty of talk. Regina didn't care. The jealous friends of his original girlfriend spread rumors about loose morals. Regina could see the whispering as she walked the hall on her new boyfriend's arm.

Regina didn't care. She got on the cheerleaders squad with his influence, which enhanced her chance of getting into one of the top colleges. She dumped him as soon as he no longer served her purpose. He came from a well-to-do family, but Regina knew that with his poor mind his high school days were his high mark. It was all down-hill for him after graduation. Regina was petite and tiny, but her plans for the future were large.

Hunger may have weakened her body but it did nothing to destroy her beauty. Early on she learned how to use that beauty. To her it was an asset, no different from her knack for math. Regina was an opportunist who used whatever talent or trait would pull her out of the poverty of her youth.

She was only sixteen when she left her birth family, the family who wallowed in their bad luck. She was sick of their whining. *Luck is created!* Regina mused, as she rode the bus out of the dusty town of her youth. She intended to create her own. An early graduation from high school because of her hard work and genius gave her the opportunity to pick from the scholarships she had been offered. Regina picked a college that was on the East Coast, the one furthest from her home town. And she never returned. It never crossed her mind to visit or even write her family. She never thought of them again.

In college she again applied herself, studying accounting, with a minor in English. The real education was social. She learned how to handle herself with the rich and powerful. While the wealthy students partied in their newly-found freedom, Regina studied them. She learned how to dress and carry herself. She became educated in fine cuisine, fashion, and the closed culture of the wealthy. She took all the money she had saved by working summers, and purchased some classic clothes. She haunted estate sales and scouted out ancient brooches and bracelets that looked inherited. Regina didn't waste her time with the political upheavals and demonstrations of her time. She followed the affluent and moved in their circles. She attended all the blue-nose functions, and volunteered for all the pet charities of the rich alumni. Regina learned to handle each crisis with grace, impressing her emotionally-charged classmates and their wealthy parents with her coolness under fire. She had plans. And she only deviated from her plan once.

His name was Daniel and the first time they met, he made her laugh—not an easy thing to do. His long blond hair and scruffy beard made his green eyes sparkle even more. In the college cafeteria, Regina went to heat up the cheap noodle soup that was her standard dinner only to find Daniel's deserted bag of popcorn in the microwave. Mumbling, she moved his food and started her own. Sitting alone in the corner she watched as a large group of students planned an anti-war demonstration. And there he stood, moving gracefully, and talking fluently to the crowd who followed his every motion. He didn't shout, nor did he need to. His sense of leadership was natural, unstudied and easy. When he spoke the others listened and because of his chiseled good looks, many of the listeners were female. *I wonder how many of those girls really care about the war!* Regina thought. She rose to get her heated soup, only to find Daniel retrieving his now cold popcorn.

And he smiled—that careless captivating smile. It tore her heart open.

"Does noodle soup have more rights than popcorn? I guess soup is considered a more serious food than corn?" he laughed. He followed her to the corner. Regina was stunned by his sudden attention. She blushed and struggled, trying to make conversation with the boy who took her breath away. Even using all her education, she found it impossible to carry the conversation. Every time she broached a serious subject, he causally threw popcorn her way. Regina couldn't keep her thoughts straight anyway—looking into those green eyes. Finally, she laughed. The reward was one of his winning grins. Before she could finish her soup, she found herself falling in love. She spent the next month walking around the campus with his arm draped around her shoulder.

They became inseparable. Daniel and Regina shared every waking moment together. The first time Daniel kissed her, her body seemed to melt. The very scent of him made her dizzy. Regina had never felt this way about anyone. She couldn't think straight when he looked at her. She was in love.

Regina couldn't care less about politics, but got caught in Daniel's passion. As cool and savvy as he was on the outside, Daniel was hot and passionate on the inside. Regina got caught in that fire. She abandoned her plans to court the wealthy. She forgot her goals of social acceptance. All that consumed her was Daniel and his warm laughter and passionate kisses.

For the rest of the year, they were everywhere together. As the weather warmed so did their relationship. Unable to bear the thought of separation, Regina followed Daniel to a summer job at the local diner of the college town. Daniel was a townie. Raised in a home just five blocks from the Ivy League college, he loved his large and loud family. It wasn't until she met his parents that she realized how middle-class he was. His love of food and earthy nature were clearly inherited from his vivacious Italian mother. Daniel's easy laugh and green eyes came from his Irish father. All of his numerous brothers and sisters had the same coloring but Daniel was the best-looking.

Sitting around a large table full of bowls of pasta and sausage,

Regina watched and realized that even the family looked up to Daniel. His siblings listened to his opinions and answered with banter and arguments, but with great respect.

"Daniel, you're going to make a great teacher!" the youngest sister commented, "Mr. Wholly can't wait until you come back!"

"Who is Mr. Wholly?" asked Regina.

Daniel grinned. "Wholly is the high school principal. He's holding a teaching job for me. When I graduate from college, I'll be going back to high school."

Regina almost choked on her bread. She couldn't believe her ears.

"You're kidding, aren't you?" Regina looked deeply into those emerald eyes. "You don't want to stick around this little town and teach school, do you?"

Daniel looked at Regina with a steady gaze, some of the sparkle leaving his eyes. "That's the plan. That's always been the plan."

Forgetting that his family was watching, Regina commented, "You can't want to stick around this town. Why, there's a whole big world out there for you to conquer. I just assumed you would be going into politics."

Daniel looked down at his plate as he stirred his food with his fork. "Why would I want to leave my family and my home? I love it here."

"I thought that you would want to go into politics—you care so much about it! Isn't that why you are majoring in political science?" Regina asked with wide eyes. She had been dreaming of their future together for a year. Regina had pictured him running for governor. She knew Daniel didn't come from wealth. She was determined to lead him to it. She imagined him rising to the top. Regina had no doubt that his good looks and charisma would land him in national politics. She envisioned him in Washington and she planned to be right beside him. Regina didn't notice that the table had gone silent.

"No, the plan has always been for me to teach history at the high school. I have always wanted to be a teacher," Daniel answered softly, as if trying to alleviate the blow the news was to Regina.

Regina didn't answer. The banter at the table continued without her attention. She was cordial, and left early to return to her dorm room. Only Daniel seemed to notice the change in her.

That night, tossing wildly in her cot, Regina dreamt of living in the small town. In her vision she was holding a baby on the porch of one of the Cape Cod homes that dotted the college town. She was older, sitting on the red brick step watching Daniel walk home from his job at the high school. In the dream a feeling of dread washed over her. Looking down, she realized she was wearing one of her mother's housecoats. Regina woke bathed in sweat. Her hands shook, as she pushed the tangled blankets from around her legs. She splashed her face with cold water in the bathroom sink and looked at herself in the mirror. She could see her eyes welling with tears. Regina knew what she had to do.

It was one of the few battles that she lost. Daniel wouldn't change. She manipulated. She threatened. In the end, she even cried. But there it was—the gap between them grew larger. It grew so large it became an abyss that neither could cross. Daniel graduated the following spring and Regina never saw him again. They had been passing each other on campus as if they were strangers. She told herself it was all for the best. She told herself that she had done the right thing. She even believed it for a while. Regina resumed her plan to find the kind of husband she needed with a vengeance. It was just before Christmas break when she met her future.

She spotted him at her roommate's party. Regina had made sure that she volunteered on the dormitory's organization committee. She made sure that she was rooming with the wealthiest girl on campus for her senior year. Wearing the borrowed silk dress that made her figure stand out, she spotted him. He was standing alone in a corner. Awkward and shy, Harrison Kagan wasn't much to look at. His thinning brown hair and round face was accentuated by the Harry Potter glasses. *Those glasses will be the first thing to go*, laughed Regina to herself. She could feel Harrison watching her as she displayed the social graces he never quite mastered. He seemed fascinated. Regina approached him and she watched the artery in his neck pulse with his anxiety.

"Hell…o." Seemed to be all he could get out as he stared at Regina. Regina smiled and his face reddened in response. She noticed that he never took his eyes off her. Reaching out, she touched his hand and introduced herself.

"M…m…y nam…me is H…h…arrison." He answered. When her smile widened, he was encouraged.

Stammering, he tried to make small talk. She was captivated by his halting speech. His dialogue was not graceful at all but full of brilliant business savvy. From Regina's first smile he was smitten.

He took her home to meet his family in the Hamptons. They never suspected that she hadn't been raised in a cultured, wealthy environment. One year after her graduation they were married and the wedding was the social event of the season. Six hundred people attended the gala outdoor wedding. None of those in attendance were related to the bride. A whirlwind tour of Europe was the wedding gift of the groom's parents. She told herself she loved him. To be honest she had a kind of affection for the bumbling genius. She tried to convince herself that she would be happy. It wasn't until that first night, the night they stayed in Paris, that she realized her heart would never heal. In bed she closed her eyes and in the midst of her husband's awkward attempts at making love, she pictured Daniel's face.

But those who want to get rich fall into temptation and a snare and many foolish and harmful desires which plunge men into ruin and destruction. For the love of money is a root of all sorts of evil, and some by longing for it have wandered away from the faith and pierced themselves with many griefs. But flee from these things, you man of God, and pursue righteousness, godliness, faith, love, perseverance and gentleness.
—*Timothy 6: 9–11*

Chapter Eight

The poor live in the present. *What will I eat today?* they ask themselves. *Will the landlord be by this afternoon?* is their nagging thought. The middle class live in the future, saving for that dream vacation or scrimping for a secure retirement. The wealthy revel in the past, often claiming a part in the accomplishment of their ancestors, and searching family history for royal blood or military prowess. The newly rich are in a special class, ashamed of the past and unsure of the future. They often bury the joy of the present in the open wounds of their endless fear.

Harrison Kagan came from a long line of wealth. His family had accumulated their fortune in steel. Rising out of the slums of Pittsburgh, generations of the Kagan family had forged an empire in the country's heated quest for building material. They diverted into publishing right before the steel market fell. Kagan Publishing now paid for the North Shore mansion in the Hamptons, as well as numerous cattle ranches, oil fields, and penthouses scattered across all the major cities in the United States and Europe.

Much to Regina's chagrin Charles Kagan, Harrison's father, seemed to be in the business of spending wealth, not accumulating it. He had allowed the business to grow stagnant. Top heavy and stodgy, its everyday operations were run by a committee of elderly men who seemed afraid to take chances or keep up with the modern world. The company had become high-brow, catering to cerebral authors of literary note or Ivy League professors pouring their vanity into textbooks their students were forced to buy. Hard-cover classics were not on the best-sellers list.

The Kagan Publishing Company might have had class, but Regina was only interested in sales and she knew that the only way was to remove Charles Kagan. She needed a plan, and it didn't take her long to devise one.

"Harrison," she casually commented, "did Charles seem a little confused to you this afternoon?"

"No, not particularly." Harrison cocked his head, as if letting the thought roll around his mind.

Regina quickly changed the subject. She wanted it to settle, like a casual thought, a seed planted.

The following month, she planned a surprise party for Charles's birthday. She laughed telling Harrison how she had told Charles it was a celebration of the company's anniversary. For weeks she cemented the details for the celebration. The orchestra and caterer were hired. Invitations were sent out. Everyone was looking forward to the formal event, prepared to surprise Charles on Saturday night. Only Charles received the phone call changing the night of the party to the previous Friday. When he arrived in black tie, Harrison was stunned.

"Where is everyone?" Charles gulped.

Regina smiled while gracefully making the mistake seem like a small one. Harrison was shocked by his father's arrival. When Charles saw the "Happy Birthday" banner that was strung across the dining room wall, the surprise was ruined.

"I received a call that the date was changed!" Charles pulled the invitation out of his vest pocket, "I know the invitation says the party is tomorrow, but I swear that someone called my office and changed the date to today!"

Regina smiled and nodded. Taking his topcoat, she shrugged her shoulders behind his back, a silent signal to Harrison that his father was clearly confused. She had made sure that the call couldn't be traced to her. In fact, Charles had no way of proving that he had ever received such a call.

Two months later, soon after arriving to spend the evening with Charles at his large ranch, Regina slipped into the kitchen. The cook had left trays of food that just needed to be heated. Charles had carefully set the oven to 300 degrees, as per the instructions. It took Regina just seconds to raise the oven temperature to 450. She was sitting on the sofa next to Charles and laughing at his latest joke when Harrison noticed the smoke billowing out of the kitchen.

Within six months of the marriage, Charles was no longer coming into the city. He was escorted everywhere by a hired nurse. Harrison was now commissioned to turn Kagan Publishing into a growing, thriving business. With eyes turned toward the future, Regina encouraged Harrison to expand. When the men who ran the company objected, she used Harrison's power to push her agenda through.

Harrison took over. At first, he found running the company exciting. He used all his political clout and savvy to expand. The company grew and extended as it acquired one small entity after another, swallowing the small and medium presses around the country. Paperback mysteries and romance novels became their biggest sellers. Regina pushed the magazines into popular entertainment and gossip mode. The sales rocketed. Supermarkets couldn't keep the tabloids in stock.

Regina took a corner office in the large New York building that the Kagan Publishing Company now owned. Regina loved every minute of pre-dawn strategy meetings and late-night dinners in the city. Her adrenaline pumped as they forced lesser companies into selling and took over the newspapers of most of the major cities in the country. Regina had no mercy. She cared little for the employees who lost their jobs or the tradition that the papers or magazines held. She loved the thrill of conquering the rich, and surprising those who thought they were safe. The more she accumulated, the more she longed for.

Harrison Kagan wasn't the same. To him it was a game, and he soon lost interest in it all. Within the first year he started missing days at the office. He preferred spending time at the country club and on the golf course. Encouraged by her energy, he slowly let Regina take over. Her business savvy was becoming legendary. She worked twelve- hour days and spent little time at the mansion she and Harrison now owned.

"Come home," Harrison begged, thinking of the prospect of spending another night with the servants. He had married her because she brought a sense of adventure into his drab life. Now he was bored and alone most of the time.

"I have that meeting with the London executives in the morning." Regina replied. If it wasn't that meeting it was another. Many nights she spent alone in the penthouse that the company kept in the city for convenience. It didn't bother her to be alone. Regina loved the feel of the satin sheets as the fireplace roared with warmth. Looking out the large window that displayed the lights of the city, she felt like a queen. Here, she could revel in the luxury of her new life and she didn't feel the need to share that sense of accomplishment with anyone, least of all Harrison. Truth be told, she found him uninteresting. His concentration on golf and the social gossip of the privileged didn't concern her. Regina only cared about her next business move, the next winning strategy.

She had shared a bed with her brothers in the shack she grew up in. She was happy to enjoy seclusion in the riches she had found. Regina wasn't worried about Harrison's begging. It was when he stopped begging that she grew suspicious. At first Regina didn't deduce anything. Besides, she was so busy with her latest acquisition that she rarely thought of Harrison. He was like a pet to her. She would indulge him with affection when she saw him, but rarely thought of him when he was out of sight. They had only been married for five years, when she felt that something was wrong.

Perhaps, I've ignored him too much; Regina thought as she discreetly hired the private detective. Within a week she knew the truth. Spreading the photos on the bed, she could almost laugh at Harrison's puppy dog eyes looking up at the tall, cool redhead. She would have laughed if it didn't put her position in such danger. Harrison had been having an affair for over a year. She was determined that she wasn't about to lose him. It was more than the riches. Regina had discovered that there was something more important to her than money. Regina had discovered power. And she was not about to give it up.

Many women would have cried or confronted their husbands with the evidence. Regina walked over to burn the report and all the photos in the fireplace. She didn't need evidence. Still, she stopped herself from burning the photos. Instead she put them in a large brown envelop and wrote the address of the redhead's husband. Dropping it in the "out" mailbox, she grinned. Now she needed a plan.

The next day, she called the office, postponing or canceling all her appointments for the week. Instead, Regina went shopping. She brought new lingerie in Neiman Marcus. She purchased the most expensive perfume at Macy's. While being driven home, she called to have the caterer deliver Harrison's favorite food. Regina approached her marital problems with the same energy and strategy as she did any other take-over.

Harrison was blown away by the attentions of his wife. He spent the week cuddled with Regina, much to the chagrin of his mistress. The tall mistress who had grown up as part of the same élite circle that the Kagans traveled in didn't have a chance. In Regina's arms Harrison forgot she existed. Regina spent a week wooing her husband back. He would never know that she knew all about his affair. His guilt made him cut his mistress off before the week ended. Regina learned a valuable lesson. *I'll never lose control again,* Regina thought, as she kissed Harrison awake. She kept her promise to herself.

A few months later, she discovered that she was pregnant with Bridget. An heir was just what Harrison had longed for. Up until now, she had dreaded the idea of a crying, puking infant. It was not what Regina wanted, but she knew it was just what she needed. Regina realized almost too late that her husband was slipping away. If she lost him, she would lose half the business or maybe all of it and Regina was determined not to let that happen. The baby was her insurance policy. He wouldn't leave her with a baby on the way. Regina was not about to let her fortune slip through her fingertips. She had given up too much and worked too hard to go back to being poor.

Regina stopped spending her nights in the penthouse. She left early and returned to find that she could get a lot of work done while the limo was stuck in traffic on the Long Island Expressway. She even started to work in her office at home, only going into the city for special meetings or conferences. She indulged Harrison's interest in social gatherings by hosting large gala affairs that became the highlight of Hampton society. Dressed in sparkling gowns that cost thousands, she hid as much of her pregnancy as she could. Regina was uncomfortable; the pregnancy slowed her down, making her feel awkward and ungainly. She was actually glad when she felt the first contraction. She wanted it to be over. She had already decided that this was the last pregnancy for her.

"It's a girl," the doctor announced, holding the crying infant up. Regina had hoped for a boy, but when she saw Harrison's delight, she knew that it was settled. She had given the Kagans their heir and her position was safe and secure.

The first thing Regina did was hire a nanny. She needed to get back to work. And while she spent most of her time at work, she never neglected her husband again. She was happy to see the deep bonding between Harrison and Bridget. She wanted to cement his heart to the family. When he wasn't out playing golf or yachting, Harrison spent all his time with Bridget.

The call came while Regina was at work. She didn't bother with the limo that was always on standby. The company helicopter whirled quickly through the air and landed on the roof of the hospital. She found Bridget sitting alone in the hallway outside the Coronary Care Unit. Only eight, Bridget ran to her mother crying.

"Mommy, I tried to wake him up. He was talking one minute, then he just fell to the ground, I shook him but he didn't wake up."

"Shh…You did well Bridget. You called 911. That was good thinking. You didn't panic. Because of you he may be all right!" Regina tried to sooth the girl who clung to her, petting the girl's hair in long gentle stokes.

She knew better. She had spoken to the doctor from the copter. Harrison had been without oxygen too long. They were doing an E.E.G. searching for brain activity. Regina knew that they weren't hopeful.

It was a massive heart attack. They couldn't revive him. At the tender age of thirty- three, Regina found that she was a widow, a widow with a multi-million dollar corporation to run. Bridget clung to her mother—through the wake and the funeral. Regina stayed close, allowing the shaken child to share her empty bed. Bridget was inconsolable.

"Do you think that he can see us? Can he see us from heaven?" asked Bridget one month after the funeral. She was struggling, falling behind in school and moping around the house. It was starting to irritate Regina. Bridget was becoming a burden. She was distracting Regina from her work.

"Don't be ridiculous!" Regina answered. "You're old enough to know that all of that is just a fairy tale. Your father is gone and you just better get used to it. He won't be the first and he won't be the last. Everybody dies. That why it's a shame to waste time wallowing around."

Bridget started to cry and it was more than Regina could bear. "You need to straighten up. Get some gumption. It's time you grew up and stopped acting like a baby and I know just the place for you."

Regina, over the tears of her daughter, made arrangements for the best prep school in the nation. *It is a shame that it is on the other side of the country,* Regina thought as she sent her only child away. *Still, Bridget has to toughen up and I need to get back to work.*

And so Bridget was sent to the best boarding school in the nation, and spent most of her summers, unwanted by her busy mother, with the friends she met there. When they were together, Regina and Bridget didn't get along. Regina had little time to spend with the daughter who grew to be a stranger. And as the gap between them grew, Bridget came to resent the mother who neglected her. Regina was always busy working on a new deal.

When Bridget returned after graduating from college, she tried to connect with her mother. Joining her mother at the breakfast table on her first day home, Bridget tried to engage her, "Mom, would you like to go shopping today. I need some new clothes and we could go to lunch while we're out."

Regina ignored her. She was distracted by a new plan, a dynamic deal.

"Don't you have any friends to hang out with?" Regina retorted, "I have no time to waste running around all day with you."

Bridget withdrew. *She has never had time for me!* she thought. *I'll never ask her to spent time with me again!*

Regina never noticed. She was planning her strategy

Kagan Publications had grown and been successful by changing their focus, but Regina knew that they had to keep up with all the new technology. She knew that the publishing world was changing fast, and traditional publishers who didn't change with the times would be going under. Most of the large publishers were clinging to the old ways She knew that with the advent of the home computer, all that was traditional in the publishing world was about to implode.

Regina attended the next board meeting with an agenda. She was determined to pull Kagan Publishing into the future.

"Gentlemen, Vanity presses had been around for years. Those with the money could print their books to show off or sell to colleagues or family. The company I want us to acquire has innovative plans on the table. It is the vanguard for affordable self-publication,"

Regina paused. Looking around, she could see the elderly faces were not sold on her plan. *What a bunch of sticks in the mud!* she thought.

Determined to convince them she continued, "I know a modern company that allows anyone who writes a book to publish their manuscript in a professional, well-bound volume. I want that company. Change is coming and I want us to be a part of that change."

The people on the board disagreed with her. Most thought that home computers were a fleeting idea that would come and go. What was this thing called the internet anyway? Regina knew better. She wasn't worried. Regina had a plan B. She knew that if she couldn't make Kagan Publishing submit to change, she could take over one of the companies that had moved quickly into the publishing world of the future.

Regina knew exactly which company she wanted and she only wanted the best. There was a glitch in her plan. The company she wanted hadn't gone public. Regina couldn't take over by a covert acquisition of stocks. The company was family owned, and the family was not inclined to sell. What she hoped would prove an incentive turned out to be a blockage.

The family owned the estate that bordered her Long Island mansion. The Coles were her next-door neighbors. Regina befriended them. She offered them more money than the company was worth. Still, the father, Anthony Cole, refused. He wanted to pass the company on to his children. Regina knew she had time, but as the interest in home computers started to grow, she knew that her time was limited. That's when it occurred to her. *If I can't take over the company with money, I may be able to find my way in with marriage,* Regina thought. The daughter who never interested her started to look more like an asset.

But despite her plans, Bridget refused. She stood on the stairs and defied Regina. She married John Laverty against Regina's will.

Regina never forgot it. Bridget's stroke had given her a golden opportunity. She watched as the Coles' company grew. *Let it grow,* she smiled as she pushed Lander into a relationship with Winnie Cole. Regina may have been disappointed by Bridget's marriage, but she was patient. The marriage of her grandson to the heir of the business she craved would unite the two companies. And Regina planned to live long enough to see that day.

He that troubleth his own house shall inherit the wind: and the fool [shall be] servant to the wise of heart.
— *Proverbs 11:29*

Chapter Nine

Love creates deep grooves when the heart is tender. So does hate. Woven deeply into the soft flesh of youth, attachments are intensely rooted, often buried so deep that they are impossible to burrow out. And those feelings never leave, although they may be denied or buried. In our later years, they float up on the aging winds of regret.

"Shh….Quiet!" whispered Lowell, with his finger on his lip.

Skylar tried to stop giggling. Peeking through the crack in the closet door, she covered her mouth and tried to hold her breath. Skylar's resolve melted as she watched what was happening in the room.

"It's her!" she whispered to her companion.

"It's the queen, come to see the crown prince!" answered Lowell.

"What's a crown prince?" whispered the tiny blonde.

"The one who is to inherit the kingdom," Lowell hissed.

Lowell and Skylar both watched as Regina swept into the room. The tailor looked up nervously. The tic in his eye quickened when he heard her first pronouncement.

"I don't like that fabric! Don't you have a finer one?" Regina asked as she rubbed the sleeve between her fingers.

"That is the finest silk we have in the shop," the balding man answered.

"Well, it will have to do," replied Regina, gazing at her beloved grandson. Lander was squirming around, bored with standing still.

"Are we done yet?" eight-year-old Lander whined. "I want to go play."

"We'll be done in just another minute," answered the tailor as he knelt, pinning the hem of the pants.

"Lander," answered Regina with an affectionate tone, "you need to stand still. The suit has to be ready by Saturday. Winnie Cole's birthday party is Sunday afternoon and you have to look perfect!"

"Aw! Why do I have to go to a girl's party anyway?" Lander complained.

Regina laughed. "There will be other boys there. But you have to make an impression. Winnie Cole is a wonderful girl and I want you to make friends with her. She lives so close to us—wouldn't it be nice if she could come over and play some time?"

"Not unless she plays baseball!" announced Lander, who was clearly happy to be released from the fitting. He donned his jeans and tee shirt, and sat down to tie his sneakers.

Regina watched him as he prepared to return to the tree house in the backyard. *Someday you'll thank me for pushing you in Winnie's direction. She is going to be a beauty,* thought the grandmother.

As the tailor left, gently closing the door behind him, a loud sneeze took both Lander and Regina by surprise. Regina quickly spanned the room and yanked the closet door open.

"Well…why am I not surprised," she announced as she watched the two children who had been leaning on the door tumble from the closet. "Little spies! Look Lander! Two little losers are spying on you."

Reaching down, Regina grabbed Lowell roughly by the shoulder.

"Ow!" Lowell screamed as she pulled him across the floor. Regina tossed him in front of Lander. She gave a withering look to Skylar, which was enough to start Skylar's tears. Lowell was now lying on the floor before Lander, who sat still and pale.

"How does it feel to have your brother and his little friend hiding and laughing at you?" Regina snarled.

Lander came to Lowell's defense quickly. "It's okay! They were just having some fun."

Regina gave Lander's comment a dismissive wave of her hand

while never removing her angry glare from Lowell. Pulling Lowell up, she stood him on the tailor's platform, until he was eye level. Shaken and pale, Lowell was silent before his attacker.

"Why are you watching your brother from behind hidden doors?" Regina shouted.

Trying to look courageous, Lowell answered, "Why is Lander getting a new suit and going to a birthday party? Why ain't I going?"

Regina laughed. A laugh that was both loud and cold. "You? Why would anyone invite you to a party?"

Lowell paled and tried to step off the platform, only to be pushed back in place by his grandmother.

Regina's eyes flashed with anger. "Look at you. How can you even compare yourself to Lander? He's the important one and don't you ever forget it!"

"And as for you," said Regina, turning her wrath upon Skylar, "you're the illegitimate daughter of a servant! If I had my way you would be gone. You're not fit to be in this house and I will get rid of you before I am through!"

Skylar cowered in the corner. The tiny blonde shook before the monster she most dreaded.

"Get out of here and don't let me see you again today or I don't know what may happen," screamed Regina with such force that spittle sprayed Skylar as she dashed from the room. Hiding behind the outer door, Skylar watched in tears as Regina continued her attack on Lowell.

"You…get it through your head that you are nothing, and if I ever find you thinking that you are on the same level as your brother Lander, I will teach you otherwise!" Regina shouted.

Regina took a deep breath, as if to steady herself. Turning to Lander, she could see how upset he was. She tried to calm her temper. "Lander, come give Granny a hug. I didn't mean to frighten you."

Lander's eyes were full of tears, as he approached Regina's open arms. Gathering Lander and rubbing his strawberry blond hair, she looked over her shoulder at Lowell who stood still on the tailor's platform with wide eyes. Her stare was full of hatred.

Why? Skylar thought as she watched from behind the door. *Why does she hate Lowell so?* Skylar sighed as she watched Lowell. He seemed determined not to cry, and shook with the effort to remain still. Climbing down, Lowell headed toward the door, trying to escape his grandmother's wrath. Pulling away from his grandmother's embrace Lander quickly followed, catching Lowell before he reached the door. Putting his arm around his twin, Lander held his brother closely, "She didn't mean it. She was just surprised. Granny loves you!"

Lowell pulled away and stared at Lander with disdain. "I don't care! I hate both of you!"

Turning and running out the door, Lowell couldn't see the look of pain on Lander's face. Lander sighed and turned to Regina. "Granny, you shouldn't have said those mean things to Lowell."

Regina, now calmed, responded, "You're right Lander. I was just surprised to find them spying on you. I'll go tell Lowell I'm sorry."

Like hell I will! Regina thought. *But I have to be more careful—I can't alienate Lander.*

Lander's smile was both quick and forgiving. Regina smiled in response as she left the room, "Now go play, Lander, while I go find your brother."

Skylar ducked behind the door as Regina swept past. She had seen the smile that Lander graced his grandmother with. Looking at Lander as he finished tying his shoelace, Skylar thought he was the most wonderful boy she had ever seen. As Lander walked past without seeing her, Skylar could feel her heart quicken.

Lowell needs me, she thought as she headed to their special place. Lowell and Skylar had a special place—down in the cottage garden—where they played hidden games. Away from the unwanted stares of Regina, and the neglect of Bridget, the two children shared imaginary games of knights and great ladies, castles and battles— childhood imaginings that whiled away the afternoons and bonded the lonely souls into a special friendship.

Skylar found Lowell sitting beneath the old oak, his face streaked with tears he had tried to rub away. Picking up a branch that lay on the ground she called out

"My Lord—we need to slay the dragon!" She moved gracefully as she waved the branch in the air like a sword. Pointing the stick at the old oak, Skylar jabbed the trunk as if attacking.

Lowell looked up and smiled at the antics of his little friend. She liked to pretend that she was a knight—forgetting that she was a girl. Skylar was a bit of a tomboy. Lowell remembered his father saying that was not surprising considering that she was being raised with two high-energy boys. He thought that it would pass once Skylar went to kindergarten. However, even now that she was in school, she preferred her friendship with Lowell. They spent hours together. In the garden of the cottage, they let their imaginations soar. They created a world where they were the heroes—ready to make the world just again.

It was a far cry from the real world that they lived in. Lowell felt ignored by the silent mother who roamed the house in seeming disinterest. He dreaded the attention of his cold and hate-filled grandmother. She never let a meeting pass without letting Lowell know that he wasn't wanted. She seemed to think that he should have never been born. His father cared for him, but he was usually at work and busy spending time with his wife. Except for Skylar, Lowell felt unloved and unwanted.

Skylar had her own pain. She sensed that she didn't really belong to the family although she didn't really understand why. She had no way of knowing that John Laverty had applied to adopt her twice. Each time, Hannah's family had raised objections, blocking the adoption. Both times, they claimed that they wanted Skylar for themselves. However, once John dropped the applications, they withdrew their request for Skylar. John suspected that Regina was somehow behind it, but had no proof. His fear of losing the little girl prevented any further attempts to adopt her. So Skylar remained a foster child.

She had no women in her life. It was clear from the beginning that Regina hated her. Bridget ignored her and no one else seemed to have time for her. Lowell was the only one she could share her little thoughts and secrets with. In the past, she had tried to befriend Lander. He was responsive, but his grandmother put an end to the friendship as soon as she got wind of it. Regina made sure that Skylar stayed away from Lander. In the absence of the love that they needed, they clung to each other. Creating a world of justice and light, they played together whenever they had the chance. Lowell watched as Skylar attacked the tree that represented the dragon.

Rising he grabbed another stick and joined in the attack.

"Regina, the fire-breathing dragon—take that!" Lowell cried as both he and Skylar stabbed the tree trunk. After a good five minutes of sword play, they both sat beneath the defeated enemy. And as reality replaced imagination, Lowell's face returned to sadness.

"Don't let the dragon defeat you." Skylar reached out and put her arm around Lowell. "Someday you will be a full knight and she will be defeated by your power."

A look of hatred crossed Lowell's face. "I will destroy her. I will destroy all of them!"

Skylar was frightened by the anger in Lowell's eyes. She had never seen her friend so distraught.

"Don't be sad. Lander will help you slay the dragon!"

Lowell laughed, a deep sardonic laugh that caused Skylar to pull away. "I don't need anyone's help. I will destroy them all!"

*

Lander rubbed his neck, irritated by the stiff white shirt. *What a stupid party*, he thought as he watched Winnie's grandmother cut the large pink and white cake. There were no good games. Everyone was too dressed up to have fun. He couldn't wait until it was all over and he could change and get back to his tree house.

Mr. and Mrs. Cole fussed over Winnie as she passed the slices of cake around the table on fancy china plates. Most of the other children were girls, and Winnie made Lander sit right next to her.

"Isn't he cute?" Mrs. Cole said. "Don't they make the cutest couple?"

Lander wanted to barf! There was something strange about Winnie's family. Lander didn't know the whole story, but he had heard that both of Winnie's parents were away at a place called rehab. They came occasionally to visit but never seemed to stay. Winnie was being raised by her grandparents and a more spoiled and silly girl Lander never knew.

Still, Granny wanted him to make a good impression, so he tried to pretend that he was having a good time. Winnie opened up a lot of girly gifts, like dolls and fancy clothes. Lander just wanted to get the heck out of there. He was thrilled when he heard the doorbell ring and watched the party end as parents picked the children up.

Where is Granny? he wondered as one by one the other guests disappeared. He was the last one there. It didn't seem to bother Winnie, who sat closer and prattled on and on about how much she liked him.

"Will you be my boyfriend?" Winnie cooed, as Lander tried to move away. Then the worst thing that ever happened to him occurred. Winnie kissed him!

Lander was about to bolt, when the doorbell rang. Granny had sent the gardener to pick him up.

"Oh, does he have to go?" Winnie whined to her grandfather.

The grandfather laughed. "He can come over anytime and play! Wouldn't you like that Lander?"

Lander didn't know what to say. He didn't plan on coming back anytime soon.

"Didn't you like the party and the cake?" asked Winnie.

"Yes," answered Lander as he tried to divert the girl's attention, afraid that she might kiss him again.

"Can I have a piece of cake to take home to my brother?" he asked the grandmother.

"Of course!" she smiled as she cut a large slice and placed it on a paper plate, "It's a shame he couldn't come. I hope he feels better soon."

Grabbing the cake, Lander ran out the door and into the car, barely escaping another show of affection from Winnie Cole.

Arriving home, he found Lowell sitting alone in the nursery.

"Here, I brought you a piece of cake," Lander stated as he placed the plate on the table before Lowell. There was no response. *I guess he's still mad*, thought Lander as he rushed into the bedroom to remove the suit. Happy to get back into his play clothes, he took the time to carefully lay the suit out on his bed. He knew how important the suit was to Regina. He had been very careful not to spill anything on it at the party. She had emphasized how expensive and impossible to clean a silk suit was. Lander was glad the whole thing was over.

*

Lowell stared at the cake. He picked up the plate and watched as Lander left the bedroom and headed toward the backyard. Going into the bedroom he looked at the silk suit that Lander had carefully laid out on the bed. Walking over, he took the cake and breaking off pieces of pink and white icing smeared the jacket and the pants with it. Lowell rubbed as much of the cake into the suit as he could. Tears streamed down his cheeks. Throwing the empty paper plate under the bed, he ran out of the bedroom. He didn't see Bridget, who watched from the hallway.

And the Lord sent Nathan to David. He came to him and said to him, "There were two men in a certain city, the one rich and the other poor. The rich man had very many flocks and herds, but the poor man had nothing but one little ewe lamb, which he had bought. And he brought it up, and it grew up with him and with his children. It used to eat of his morsel and drink from his cup and lie in his arms, and it was like a daughter to him. Now there came a traveler to the rich man, and he was unwilling to take one of his own flock or herd to prepare for the guest who had come to him, but he took the poor man's lamb and prepared it for the man who had come to him." Then David's anger was greatly kindled against the man, and he said to Nathan, "As the Lord lives, the man who has done this deserves to die...
2 Samuel 12: 1–31

Chapter Ten

In the cold of night, the monsters come. What is in the closet, or under the bed? We are too afraid to look. We pull our blankets over our heads, and our imaginations take flight. What we dream in the lonely hours is always worse than any truth. Always, our greatest fear is to be alone, alone and forgotten. Will someone come and open the closet door or look under the bed? Or will we have to face our monsters alone? It is so dark alone in the night.

Yet the light of love is always wrapped around us. Its warmth is only held at bay by the nightmares of our own hearts. The Father always waits. He allows us to stumble and stub our toes in the shadows of our own fears. He knows that it is only after the hours of darkness we will open our eyes to the break of day.

Crouching, Winnie and Lander silently stalked the hedges of the garden. They could hear the others playing beyond the gate. As they stealthily made their way to the garden gate, they had filled their pockets with rocks gathered from the gravel path. Their intended victims were unaware of the impending danger. Lander and Winnie reached the gate. With quick glances over the solid wood gate, Lander scanned the garden.

He could see Lowell and Skylar kicking the soccer ball back and forth. They were totally unaware of Winnie's and his presence. Lander looked over at Winnie, who waited for his signal. With a nod, they rose in unison and threw the first rock. Completely taken by surprise, Skylar screamed and Lowell ducked behind the tree. Brazen, Winnie and Lander pummeled them with one rock after another.

"Revenge!" shouted Lander, as Winnie laughed. Two hours before, they had been the victims of the latest battle in the ongoing "war" between the pairs. Lowell and Skylar had not only attacked the tree house with a barrage of missiles, but had removed the ladder that was the only means of escape. And while the walls of the tree house offered some protection, the garden gave more room to break away from the ongoing attack.

Behind the tree, Lowell collected as many rocks as he could. Filling his pockets, he fired back at his brother and the girl next door. Skylar lay low behind some bushes, unable to move as Winnie's continuous missiles were just missing her head each time she rose to look.

"Take that!" Winnie yelled.

Skylar determined that Winnie must have an unlimited arsenal of rocks in her pocket. Ducking and weaving, Skylar made her way to Lowell behind the large apple tree and collected some rocks of her own. She joined Lowell in a battle strategy of throw and duck as they responded to the barrage of rocks. Rocks bounced off the tree in an attempt to hit the intended victims.

The garden gate opened and, emboldened by the success of their apparent attack, Winnie and Lander stepped out in the open as Lowell and Skylar threw as many rocks as they could their way.

Ducking behind bushes and trees, the two invaders got closer and closer to the apple tree and their aim grew more accurate with each step.

Lowell made a strategic decision and, emerging from behind the tree, ran straight to the enemy line, with both hands firing rocks. Skylar followed his lead and ran right behind him. Surprised by the move, Lander hesitated. Winnie didn't. Rising up in full view of the counter-attack, she hurled a large rock right at Skylar.

"Geronimo!" she screamed as the rock flew through the air. It glazed Skylar's forehead right in the corner, knocking her to the ground.

The battle stopped suddenly as the three children watched Skylar hit the ground.

There was blood everywhere. Lowell ran up to his companion. Sitting beside her, he lifted her head and placed it on his lap. The head wound was deep and gushing blood. Taking the tail of his shirt, Lowell placed even pressure on the wound. Skylar moaned unconsciously, as Lander and Winnie rushed to her aid.

"Better get Dad!" Lowell shouted. "It looks bad!"

Lander didn't hesitate and turning ran quickly toward the house. Winnie's eyes filled with tears. "I didn't mean to…"

She crouched and rubbed Skylar's arm.

It seemed forever before their father arrived. Scooping Skylar up in his arms, he reached the end of the driveway just in time to hear the ambulance arrive.

Jumping in the back of the ambulance with the small blonde on a gurney, he looked back at the three children and shouted, "Get back up to the house! I'll deal with you three later!"

Sitting in the parlor, the three waited for an hour to hear if Skylar was okay. Their father arrived in a taxi, and Skylar, with her head wrapped in gauze, was beside him.

"Margaret!" John Laverty shouted for the housekeeper. "Take Skylar up to her room. She needs to rest. She got three stitches in her forehead."

Margaret helped the dazed girl up the staircase.

Turning, John Laverty approached the three children who had been waiting.

"Which one of you hit Skylar with the rock?" he asked.

Lowell looked away. Winnie hesitated, and as she opened her mouth to admit her guilt, she was shocked by Lander's sudden pronouncement.

"I did!" he answered.

Both Lowell and Winnie turned in surprise.

"I threw the rock that hit her," he continued.

"Well, it was a stupid thing to do!" shouted John. "And such a stupid action cannot go unpunished. You're grounded for a week and there will be no more rock throwing. Do you understand?"

"Yes sir," answered Lander, looking down at the carpet.

"Now go and apologize to Skylar," John continued. "She really got hurt. In fact, she will probably have a scar."

Lowell and Winnie said nothing as they watched Lander walk slowly up the stairs to Skylar's room.

Turning back, John stared at the two of them. "It may have been Lander's rock that hit Skylar, but you were all throwing rocks. There will be no more of it—got me?"

Winnie nodded in agreement and headed quickly out the door and across the lawn. She was glad to get home with her reputation still intact. *Why did Lander take the blame?* she wondered. *Oh well, it doesn't matter,* she mused. *At least I'm not being blamed!*

*

Lander tiptoed into Skylar's room. The lighting was dimmed and she lay quietly in the canopy bed that made her room so much like a fairy tale. The walls were a soft pink and the furniture was white with gold touches. The curtains, which were white with pink roses, were drawn to keep out the sunlight. The walls of the room held numerous shelves lined with stuffed animals and long-haired dolls.

Such a sissy room! He thought as his eyes adjusted. *She looks so small in the bed.* Lander approached quietly, hoping that she would be asleep and he could make his escape.

"Hello," she whispered quietly.

"Does it hurt?" Lander asked as she reached up to touch the injury hidden behind the gauze.

"No, not so much! The doctors put it to sleep with a needle," she responded.

"I'm sorry," Lander said. "I'm sorry I hit you with that rock."

Skylar hesitated and stared at her visitor, "I thought it was Winnie who hit me."

"No, it was me. I'm glad it doesn't hurt," Lander whispered and suddenly wondered why they were both whispering.

"The doctor said that it will probably leave a scar."

"Not a big one. I have a bigger one on the back of my head. I got it when I was a baby. You can't see it because it is covered by hair," answered Lander optimistically.

Skylar gave a weak smile. "I guess I can wear bangs."

She yawned, putting her hand to her mouth.

"Guess you're tired." Lander rose to leave. "I promise never to throw rocks at you anymore."

"Okay," Skylar answered as she closed her eyes in sleep. *It was like hitting a little bird,* he thought as he closed her bedroom door behind him.

*

Lowell felt all alone with Skylar injured. Lander tried to interest him in a game of Mario brothers, but he couldn't concentrate. Lander always won the video games anyway. *There's no use trying to beat him at his favorite games,* thought Lowell as he watched his brother delight in the bouncing figures. They were both confined to the playroom. It was a sunny and mild day and Lowell longed to be outside. Being stuck in a room with the twin he hated so was not his idea of fun. They finally escaped each other's company when they were called to the dining room for dinner.

Right after dinner, Lowell snuck into Skylar's room.

"You awake?" he asked as he spanned the room to her bed.

Skylar opened her eyes and smiled, "Yes, I had a good nap. My head doesn't hurt so much and I even had a good dream."

"Oh yeah, what ya dream about?" asked Lowell.

"I had a dream that Lander came to see me and told me that I was his friend and that he was sorry about throwing rocks," she answered.

Lowell could feel the anger rising. *Lander has plenty of friends,* he thought, as his heart pounded in his chest. *Why does he want my only friend?*

The thought of Lander talking to Skylar made his stomach churn. *Lander has everything—can't he leave something or someone for me!*

"That is a dream!" he answered. "Imagine the crown prince saying that's he's sorry. It must be a dream—it would never happen in real life!"

Lowell sat on the edge of Skylar's bed and took her hand. "You know that I'm your only friend, don't you? We have to stick together."

"Yeah, we'll always be together," answered the small blonde. "You're my best friend. Too bad we can't throw rocks any more. I'm sure we could beat Winnie and Lander. Teach them a lesson!"

"It's funny," Skylar mused. "I could swear that Winnie was the one who threw the rock. In the dream, Lander said he threw it."

"He did throw it. I saw him and he threw it hard!"

"Do you think he really wanted to hurt me?" asked Skylar as tears formed in her eyes.

"Yes," groaned Lowell. "He's always hurting people. But don't you worry. We'll get back at the crown prince. We'll teach him!"

"I promised Dad that we wouldn't throw rocks anymore," sighed Skylar.

"Well, you didn't promise anything about this!" answered Lowell as he pulled a pea shooter out of his pocket.

*Anger is cruel and fury overwhelming, but who
can stand before jealousy?*
—Proverbs 27: 3–5

Chapter Eleven

Outside my window, the leaves of a red maple quiver in the autumn wind. A squirrel gathers supplies as flocks of sparrows land for a quick rest. In a remarkable pattern the tiny birds then soar together into the sky to head south. One shivering bird, clinging to a barren branch, remains. Leaves blow frantically in the wintry wind. Yet, the ruffled sparrow clings to the branch, perhaps unwilling or unable to join his kind in the journey to warmth. So it is with the jealous heart. Cold, it would rather die than soar with others.

Lander could feel his heart pounding. Lowell had confronted him so suddenly with the plan. Right before the test, at the teacher's request, Lander was handing out the answer sheets. As Lander passed, Lowell whispered. Too shocked to answer, Lander just continued down the aisle. His heart quickened as he sat back down in his desk. The instructions that the teacher gave for the test became a garbled drone, as the whispered request for help played over in his mind.

Lander had stayed up late last night studying. This was the first test of the new school year. High school felt strangely new and uncomfortable. He had left most of his friends behind, and the ancient halls of the prep school were the total opposite of the modern private school both he and Lowell had attended. Yet, he was excited by the change. Lander was anxious to try out for the outstanding teams in this new school. Greenbrier Academy had the top football team in the state. After years of playing Pop Warner, Lander was excited about learning from the well-known coach of Greenbrier's team. This afternoon was the tryout and cramming for the English test had helped. It had steadied his nerves by giving him something else to focus on.

Now Lowell wanted to him to share his answers. Lander had never cheated on anything before. He didn't want to now. Lowell sat right next to him, tapping his pencil on the desk as Mr. Barton passed out the test papers. Lander could feel the anxiety building up. *Why didn't Lowell just study last night, instead of fooling around?*

They were given thirty minutes to complete the answer sheet. You had to mark the correct multiple choice in, darkening the tiny circles. It only took Lander fifteen minutes to complete. The answers were all contained in the chapter he had studied last night. He only paused to think about one question. He could hand his paper in and leave. It was what he wanted to do. He could feel Lowell glaring, his apprehension palpable as he fingered his test sheet. Lander could feel the color and warmth rising to his face. Lowell was expectant, waiting for his help.

Lander felt the palms of his hands moisten as he slid his answer sheet over to the edge of the desk. Glancing over, he watched as Lowell copied the pattern of marks on his sheets. Lowell heard the footsteps of the teacher before Lander, just as he finished his replication. He quickly turned and wrapped his arm around his paper. Lander glanced over at Lowell's desk just as his pen slipped away and off his desk. His eyes nervously scanned around as he bent over to retrieve his ballpoint. However, it was the teacher who picked up the rolling pen.

"Can I see you outside, in the hall, Mr. Laverty?" he asked in a muted tone.

Which Mr. Laverty does he mean? wondered Lander. His question was answered by the icy look that Mr. Barton was giving him. Following the middle-aged man out into the hallway, Lander could sense the glaring looks of those students who remained burn through his back. He knew that he was going to pay the price for Lowell's poor study habits.

"I'm disappointed in you," Mr. Barton said. "I expected better of you."

"I'm sorry sir," answered Lander, not wanting to compound his mistake by denial.

"You know, of course, that you will receive a zero for this test. And the principal will have other penalties in mind. We do not tolerate cheaters in this school. Now, please collect your things and go to the office while I call your parents." Mr. Barton shook his head in apparent disgust.

Collecting his things from the classroom, Lander noticed that Lowell avoided eye contact with him as he walked up the aisle and out to the principal's office. It didn't surprise him. Lowell was avoiding a similar fate. Waiting for his father to arrive seemed like the longest thirty minutes Lowell had ever experienced. He could hear the classes changing as he sat in the wooden chair just outside the principal's office. Lander felt like everyone passing by the glass door of the office was looking at him.

A cheater, they know I am a cheater! he imagined as he waited. Only the arrival of his father, pulled from teaching his own class in public school, ended his embarrassment. Humiliation took its place. Lander couldn't look his father in the eye. His father had always stressed the importance of honesty. *He's been through so much. How could I let this happen?* Lander thought as they both entered the principal's office. He tried to look calm although his heart was beating at double the normal rhythm.

The principal was curt and direct. Cheating would not be tolerated and the punishment would be swift and severe. Greenbrier Academy had a reputation to maintain and the quality of its graduates had never included cheaters and never would.

"Do you have anything to say for yourself?" John Laverty asked as he looked quizzically at his son.

"No, sir." Lander answered. He couldn't look at his father. He couldn't bear the disappointment he imagined he would see in his eyes.

"I know you studied last night for the test. You never had any trouble with English. Are you sure there isn't something you want to say in your defense?" asked John.

"No, sir," he answered as he looked up and saw a look of bewilderment on his father's face. *How could I have embarrassed him like this? He's a teacher himself.* Rubbing his moist hands against his pant legs, Lander sighed. He could never betray his brother. He remained silent as his punishment was discussed.

Lander was expelled from the academy. The walk to the car was silent. There would be no famous coach, no football tryout. Lander could barely hold back the tears.

"I know you studied hard for this test. Can you tell me why you felt the need to cheat?" asked John on the drive home.

Lander didn't answer. He knew that his father assumed that he was the one looking for answers.

"I don't know," Lander swallowed hard.

"Well, it looks as if you blew your chance. You'll be coming to public school with me in the future. I wouldn't want to be the one that tells your grandmother." John Laverty shook his head in disgust. "I would have rather you have lower marks—like Lowell. At least he doesn't cheat to get ahead."

Lander looked out the window as the scenery flew by. He didn't want his father to see the tears that were forming in his eyes.

"I'm sorry, Dad," Lander gulped. "It was a stupid thing to do."

"Well, at least the principal was kind enough not to include it in your record. It will look like you decided to withdraw from the academy for personal reasons. It was kind of him and I think that he did it because I'm a teacher and you never got in trouble before. I hope you learned your lesson and that nothing like this ever happens again."

*

Lander hung his head as Regina ranted. "How could you be

stupid enough to get caught?"

He didn't know what to say.

"I have some pull," announced Regina, "I will call and get you back in Greenbrier. I'll make a large donation. You'd be surprised how forgetful the administration can become when a new building is donated."

"No, let it be. I shouldn't have done what I did. I'll do better in public school," he promised as both Lowell and Skylar arrived from the two different school buses that dropped them off at the end of the drive.

He looked at Lowell who watched the scene playing out before him without comment. *Why doesn't he speak up and tell the truth?* Lander wondered.

"You'll go with me in the morning and enroll," announced John Laverty, as Regina banged around in anger.

"You might as well take the both of them!" she shouted. "I'm not paying for that one to go to a private school, while Lander goes to public!"

Lowell's face blanched. "Why should I have to give up the academy? I didn't do anything wrong!"

Lander couldn't believe his ears. How could Lowell deny everything and just let him take the heat?

"You'll both go to the same school," announced Regina as she looked at Lander with disdain, "Maybe there you'll learn not to be so stupid. Maybe you could learn how to get away with cheating."

John slammed his newspaper down in disgust. "I think the whole point is to be honest."

"Okay, then," Regina answered, watching the anger grow on Lowell's face. "I honestly can't see why I should spend my money for one boy to go to a private school alone."

Stomping out of the room, she slammed her door for dramatic effect, but grinned to herself. *I know that little twerp has something more to do with this whole thing. He doesn't fool me,* she thought.

*

Skylar watched in disbelief as Lander said nothing to help his brother. *I don't believe it. How can he let Lowell be pulled out of school for his dishonesty?*

"Dad, don't let her do this," Lowell cried.

"What do you expect me to do?" John answered, turning away his gaze.

"Go talk to her! Why should I be taken out of Greenbrier? I didn't do anything wrong. I don't want to change schools." Lowell grabbed his father's arm and turned him to face him.

Pulling away, John Laverty walked away. "There's nothing I can do about it. I'm not going to waste my time talking to your grandmother. She never listens anyway."

"You're afraid of her. You won't speak up because you're afraid of her," accused Lowell, as he followed his father out of the room.

Bridget sat quietly in the chair as the argument continued. She didn't respond to any of the turmoil, but her lips tightened when Lowell accused John of being a coward. No one noticed the tiny response.

The argument continued, but the words became muddled as they left the room.

Lander sat still as a stone. Lost in his thoughts, he barely noticed Skylar as she stared at him. It wasn't until she spoke that he looked up at her.

"How can you just sit there and let Lowell be punished because of what you did?" she asked scornfully.

Lander stared at her for a few minutes. "You don't know the whole story—so just leave it alone."

"Well, tell me the whole story. You know that if you asked your grandmother she might change her mind. She always does whatever you want," Skylar answered. "I'd like to know how one brother can leave another brother hanging, without lifting a hand to help him."

Lander grinned. "That's a good question!"

"You're the one who cheated. Why should Lowell be punished?"

she asked.

Skylar stood waiting—waiting for a response that could explain Lander's actions, but there was no answer.

Lander looked away, and then rose to leave. She watched him as he walked to his room without looking back. *I don't believe him!* Skylar thought.

Shaking her head, she went to look for Lowell. Someone had to comfort him. Skylar found him alone in the kitchen. Lost in thought, he looked angry.

"How are you?" she whispered as he looked up.

"Not good," he complained. "I never expected to be punished for what Lander did."

Crossing the room, Skylar, who was usually shy, surprised herself by putting her arm around Lowell.

"I can't believe it either. I tried to talk Lander into speaking out for you. He just ignored me. You know that she would listen to him. If he asked your grandmother, she would let you stay at Greenbrier."

Looking down, Lowell whined, "Not even my father will defend me. He's afraid of the old biddy. My old man is nothing but a coward."

Skylar's blond hair brushed across his face as she tried to comfort him. He could smell her shampoo. Lowell had never noticed how good she smelled until she sat so close.

"Skylar," he whispered as he rose, "you're the only one who cares about me. The only friend I have. Putting his hands on both of her shoulders, he placed her right in front of him. Pulling her close he hugged her tightly, as he whispered in her ear.

"I don't know what I would do without you. You're my only friend. The only one I can trust."

Pulling back Lowell kissed her—gently.

Shocked by her first kiss she struggled and pulled away.

"I'll always be your friend. We grew up together."

And you're growing so nicely! he thought as he watched her blush.

"Sorry, I didn't think. I'm just so upset about everything." he answered.

Her face softened. "It's okay. I understand. Let's forget about it."

"You and I will always be friends. You're the only one I can depend on," Lowell answered as he walked away.

Skylar touched her lips as he left. She was quivering.

*

When Lowell entered the room they both shared, Lander winged a book at his head. Ducking to the left, Lowell laughed as it hit the door. "What's the matter big brother? First time you ever got in trouble?"

"You should have spoken up—why didn't you?"

"Do I look like a dope?" laughed Lowell, as he sat on his bed. "Besides, you never get in trouble—you can take the hit."

Lander shook his head. "I guess I just never expected you to pull something like that."

"And I think I got an 'A' to top it all off. Too bad it won't count for anything. She's sending me to public school along with you. The old man isn't going to do anything about it."

"You're getting just what you deserve!" answered Lander, "But what about me? I only helped you because you begged."

"Don't worry. I hear public school girls are hotter anyway." Looking over with a smirk, Lowell continued, "Winnie Cole goes to public!"

So from that time he sought opportunity to betray Him.
—*Matthew 26:15–17*

Chapter Twelve

Many people dread autumn. It brings short days. It heralds the end of summer fun, and long warm days. To those who hate fall it seems the end of things. I always thought of it as a beginning, perhaps because it conjures memories of a new school year, a fresh start. With fallen leaves that crackle beneath my feet, I remember football games, holidays, and visions of a first love that grew warm on chilly strolls through a college campus.

The autumn of life is the same for me. There is no dread, just delight, as grandchildren come into the world, and dreams are fulfilled. Perhaps it is because, slower now, I can delight in the first wood burning fire of the season. I can sit beside the fire and know that as the wood burns it provides warmth for those around it. Wood has to be aged and dry to burn.

John shepherded the group into the bleachers, first Winnie, followed by Lowell, Skylar, himself, and Bridget. He kept his wife close. Bridget smiled as he held her hand. She could feel John's warmth through the glove that kept the biting wind from chilling her. *His warmth has always been with me,* she thought as she looked at him. He had spent years talking quietly and softly, unaware of the way his words had soothed her soul. Bridget had improved slowly over the years. She was responsive and loving, yet still refused to speak. John held her gloved hand and she smiled.

Even if I never speak it doesn't matter, she thought as he smiled back. Bridget felt alive, heart and soul. She managed to show her love in so many non-verbal ways. Ever since she had returned to the marital bed, she had worked toward being a loving wife and caring mother. She had been so angry at John, angry that he returned her to the childhood home she had fought to leave. He seemed so weak, a plaything to her mother. However, when he stood up to her mother about raising Skylar, she had seen his strength. She had seen the man.

There were times she got lost, lost in a world that was separate from others. She felt the mood as it came upon her. She would become withdrawn, but those moments were growing further apart and of less duration. They had weathered the storm. Bridget felt a sense of contentment that had eluded her for so long.

It's hard to believe that it's been eighteen years, she thought, watching as the players took the field. Lander, the quarterback this year, led the pack. Scouts were in the stadium, watching her son, whose reputation had reached the ears of the colleges. Lander's future seemed assured. If he did well today, with his marks, he was bound to be offered a scholarship to one of the Ivy League colleges.

Bridget was so proud of the way he had developed despite Regina's influence. Lander loved his Granny, as he called her. She had a special love for him. *Her love can be toxic,* she thought as he watched the team set up formation for the game. Despite her love, Lander seemed to be a well-rounded boy.

Bridget clung to her husband. She felt animated, excited about the game. The cold didn't bother her. She felt so warm beside John.

"Here's some hot chocolate." Skylar offered her a steaming cup. The young girl had filled thermoses and gathered blankets before they left. There was a time, early on, when Bridget had resented Skylar. She had seen the way Hannah looked at John. Deep inside, she sided with Regina, hoping her mother would fire the nanny.

She had been at her weakest at the time, insecure in her ability to be a wife or a mother. A dark cloud had covered her mind, making it impossible for her to imagine a fulfilled life. It was unlikely to her that John would be content with a wife who couldn't share his life. She gave up. Yet, when Hannah gave her life for her child, something had snapped in Bridget.

She helped me understand the deepness of love, thought Bridget. Hannah had shown her the eternity of a love so profound that it overcame the trials of this life. She had heard of that kind of love before. Love so deep that it gave its own life to save others. That is when she pushed the dark cloud away. She was loved and she remembered that love. It was a love she had been told about as a child. The day that Hannah died, she had started to talk to that love. She had started to pray.

"Are you warm enough?" John asked as he pulled her closer.

"Yes," she answered in her mind alone. She had, long ago, given up speaking. She had decided that the stress of trying to speak had been a big part of her depression. Things were easier now, now that she had accepted being mute. And she had discovered so many ways to speak—so many non-verbal ways to share. It no longer troubled her.

"Oh! You know what I forgot," John announced as he stood up. "I forgot the cushions for the seats and the blankets. No wonder we are all so cold." Turning, he continued, "Come on, girls, come back to the car and help me carry the cushions and blankets back before the game starts. Lowell, watch over your mother."

Winnie and Skylar rose to help him. They didn't want to miss the first play either.

"Are you okay, Mom?" Lowell asked as he moved to sit beside her. Bridget smiled.

Ever since being a toddler, Lowell had sat and talked to his mother. He used her as a sounding board for all his plans and thoughts. He viewed her as safe. In the past, his attention was welcome. Bridget had felt lost in the lonely world she had accepted. His childhood babbling had penetrated the dark cloud that covered her heart. First at her feet and later beside her, he poured his thoughts, both good and bad, as he sat. She had spent hours listening to his childish babble. She enjoyed his silly plans and games. He made her feel alive, a part of something.

However, as he grew older, Lowell's plans had become darker, his stories full of hate. He was so angry, so full of the need for revenge. He resented the family, especially his brother. It was a deep pain, a pain that cut his very soul. He wanted revenge, and getting back at Regina and Lander consumed him. In his pain, he seemed to forget all the people in his life that loved him. He never talked about the father who tried to reach out to him. He never mentioned Skylar who was constantly by his side. He never seemed to credit the very mother he was talking to. The pain he felt obsessed him. His pain had frightened her at times.

"Look, just two rows in front of us—there's the scout for Duke," pointed Lowell. Bridget watched as a dark shadow seemed to cover Lowell's face. "Maybe I'll just put a good word in for my big brother. Of all the colleges considering a scholarship, that's the college he really wants to attend."

Bridget watched as Lowell walked down two bleacher steps and shook the older man's hand, introducing himself. She felt her heart jump as he smiled. A sense of foreboding sent a chill up her back.

"My brother Lander has talent. And it's so good for you to come out and spot him, despite the knee injury. I know he can overcome it with his great attitude," grinned Lowell.

"Injury? I wasn't aware of any knee injury," replied the grey-haired scout.

"Oh, it's all hush-hush, of course, don't want to let the opposing team know his weakness!" Lowell laughed.

Bridget couldn't believe her ears. Lander had no injury. *Why does he hate Lander so!*

Unable to stop him, Bridget watched as the scout got up and left. Lowell, returning to his seat, smiled. Looking at Bridget, he laughed. "Guess he had to go! Oh look, here's Dad and the girls, just in time for the game."

*

Sitting on the warm cushions and with the thick blankets covering their laps, Lowell wrapped his arm around Skylar. Her blond hair was tucked into a woolen cap as wisps of flaxen curls fell, framing her face. Her brown eyes glowed with happiness as she glanced at Lowell. They had been seeing each other publicly since Skylar turned sixteen three months ago. Secretly the bond had been growing since the day Lander had been expelled from Greenbrier. The deepening friendship had led to meetings in the cottage garden. Kissing had replaced the sword games, and grown into passionate necking.

Lowell had convinced Skylar to keep their meetings clandestine because of her age. Now that she was sixteen, they had begun to openly date. Unaware of the previous rendezvous, John and Bridget seemed pleased with the relationship. And Skylar was head over heels in love with Lowell. *I could drown in his dark eyes*, she thought as she watched his shining black hair being blown by the wind. She felt like she belonged, finally belonged to someone.

Lowell made her feel loved, secure. Skylar had felt like an unwanted outsider all her life. Regina never missed a chance to let her know that it was only charity that kept her in the family. She never failed with cutting remarks and cool glances to remind her that she didn't want her. The sense of rejection that both Lowell and she had felt growing up had been the glue that bonded them together. *With his arm around me I feel safe and loved.* Skylar moved closer to him.

The first quarter was a back and forth affair. First one team was ahead, then the other. When Lander ran the touchdown that tied the score, Skylar jumped in excitement. Looking over at Lowell and Winnie, who had remained seated, she felt a strange queasiness in the pit of her stomach. *They don't seem to be even watching the game*, she thought. Every time she looked over, they seemed to be looking at each other.

The third section ended with the opposing team making the only score of the quarter. It looked as if the other team, known for their great defense, might keep the home team from making any distance. Each time someone from the home team got the ball, they were quickly tackled by the opposing team. The fans seemed a little defeated as they went into the final quarter.

Looking over, Skylar could swear that Lowell and Winnie were holding hands beneath the blanket. While his one arm remained draped over her shoulder, she couldn't help but notice the small movements beneath the plaid stadium throw. *It's just my imagination.* She tried to push the thought from her mind. *Winnie is in love with Lander. Why am I so insecure?*

The fourth quarter was almost over. There was little more than a minute to play. Some of the spectators had started to pack up, ready to beat the crowd to the parking lot. It would be their first loss of the season. Suddenly, Lander now playing as Cornerback stripped the Greenbrier quarterback, scooped up the ball, and rumbled 22 yards for what became the game-winning score. The crowd erupted and stood up with joy.

As the crowd roared, Bridget grew so excited to see Lander cross the line that she jumped up and yelled, "Yes, Lander!"

John, who had jumped to his feet enthusiastically beside her, turned in shock. *Did I really hear her?* his mind screamed as the crowd roared.

Bridget looked over with tears in her eyes. "Yes! Lander!" she repeated.

John wept as he held her. She had spoken, with words that she meant to say.

A miracle! he cried.

"I love you," were the next words she whispered in his ear.

*

"I'll get Mom down to the car," John announced as the cheers subsided.

"Why don't you help Dad carry all the things back?" asked Lowell, looking at Skylar. "I'll bring Winnie down to the locker room. I'm sure Lander will want share this victory with his girl."

Skylar sensed something else. Perhaps it was the way Winnie smiled at Lowell, or the self-satisfied smirk that cornered his mouth. Whatever it was, the feeling that something was not quite right was overpowering. After loading up the car, she made a quick decision.

"I think I'll just run and join the others in congratulating Lander," Skylar said, as she headed back toward the bleachers.

Walking the darkened hallway that led to the locker room was eerie. The industrial grey paint of the cement walls and floor lent a depressive gloom to the long walk. The dim lights mounted on the wall were not the best illumination. She could hear the joyous cheers of the winners in the distance. It was the whispers that were so much closer that caught her attention.

"You're so beautiful!" a deeply masculine voice whispered. The passionate strain was so familiar that Skylar stopped in her tracks. *It's coming from the side hallway,* she realized. Afraid of what she already knew in her heart, Skylar took the few steps needed to see who was there. *Oh my God!* her heart cried as she placed her hand over her mouth to keep from screaming.

Lowell had her pressed against the wall. Winnie, tall and dark, seemed to melt into him as he kissed her passionately. Intent in their fervor, they pawed at each other while the kiss lingered and deepened. They never saw her. They didn't notice her sharp inhalation of breath. They didn't hear the sound of her feet as she turned and ran toward the locker room. She could hear the cries of victory growing louder as she approached the last turn before the locker room door.

Skylar couldn't think. She didn't know where she was going. She just had to get away and knew she couldn't go back, back to where they were. Tears blurred her vision as she made the turn to the last length of hallway. The lighting was dim. The hot tears became blinding as she quickened her pace. She didn't expect to hit anything. She didn't see him there. Running right into him, Skylar had to grab hold of him to keep from falling. However, as Lander wrapped his arms around her, instinctively protecting her from harm, her legs became like rubber. Skylar started to crumble. It was Lander who held her close and kept her from hitting the floor.

"Skylar, what's wrong?" he asked. Her tears flowed so heavily that she couldn't see him clearly.

"Lowell!" was all she could whisper.

"What about Lowell?" he asked as he led her to a bench on the side of the hallway.

"Lowell—he was kissing Winnie!" she cried. Looking up, she could see the question in his eyes. Then, he smiled.

"Oh so you saw Lowell kiss my girl and you got jealous, huh?" his smile broadened.

"Yes, he was kissing her. And she...she was kissing him back!" Skylar laid her head on Lander's shoulder and wept.

"Silly girl," Lowell was probably just excited about the victory—I'm sure it was just a little victory kiss!" laughed Lander.

Pulling away, he ran his fingers through her blond curls and wiped her tears away with his two thumbs.

"You know that we have all been close friends for years. It's only natural to share our emotions. I'm shocked that you are so jealous, but Winnie and I have been going steady for over a year. There's nothing for you to worry about."

Looking up, Lander whispered, "And here they come. Don't let them know how suspicious you are. I won't say a word!"

As Lander gently straightened her hair and wiped her face with his cloth, she looked up and saw Lowell and Winnie approaching.

"Smile now!" Lander said. As Skylar looked into his green eyes for direction and strength, she noticed the kind light in them.

Keep your heart with all vigilance, for from it flow the springs of life.
—*Proverbs 4:23*

Chapter Thirteen

When we are younger, we assume that everyone means well. When we see a cruel act we excuse the perpetrator as unaware, or lashing out in pain. It surprises us to find evil. With age we learn better. As our innocence dies, we suddenly know that there are those who do evil on purpose -for personal gain or mere vindictiveness.

It is a cruel lesson that comes to all at some point in life. Discernment breaks our heart. Yet, from the ashes of this knowledge comes true wisdom. We learn to step back, and watch. We are a little hesitant to give our heart to another. Our childhood has ended and maturity teaches us to be wary.

Skylar allowed Lander to direct her. She was in no state to confront Lowell and her raw pain was more then she could express. It seemed easier to yield to Lander's kindness than to depend on her own sense of betrayal.

"Hey," yelled Lowell, as he and Winnie approached Lander and Skylar, "should I be worried about you hugging my girl?"

"Yes!" replied Lander jokingly. "I'd steal her away if I didn't already love Winnie!" Pulling away from Skylar, Lander rose up and grabbing Winnie in his arms, asked, "How did you like the game?"

"You were great!" Winnie smiled as she covered him with kisses, "The town hero. Why, I bet that I'll have to keep an eye on you. All the girls will want you now."

Lowell walked over to Skylar with a curious look in his eyes. He seemed to be scrutinizing her. She turned away. She didn't want him to see the pain in her eyes. He seemed jumpy, as if he were worried about her strange mood.

Skylar had seen him like this before—whenever he was about to lie. Lowell had a habit of bending the truth every time it suited him. He would mix the lie with just enough truth to make it believable. She had asked him about it on the occasions when she witnessed his dishonesty and he had laughed.

"A little fib that makes someone feel better never hurts," was his reply to her inquiry. Skylar had the sense that she was about to witness one of those "little fibs."

It's the logistics, she thought. *They don't make sense. How did I arrive before him and Winnie when they started out way before me?* Skylar waited. She knew the lie was coming.

"Winnie and I ran into a few of the other players and stopped to talk. I guess you passed right by us," announced Lowell.

Looking up, Skylar noticed the change in Lander's eyes. His face became drawn and serious.

"That's funny. I was the first player to leave the locker room. And I ran right into Skylar. What players did you meet?" Lander asked.

Lowell got a strange look in his eye as he glanced from Lander to Skylar. Always quick on his feet, he responded, "Oh, did I say players? I meant former players—alumni. They were in love with your last-minute save, big brother, and I got to bask in your glory."

Skylar looked at Lander. She could read his face and knew that he didn't buy it. However, he smiled and covered his feelings. She noticed that he removed his arm from around Winnie. *Oh, how I wish those arms were around me again!* Shocked by her thoughts, she looked away. Her stomach cramped as Lowell took her hand and they started to walk out toward the exit. She didn't want to be with him. Skylar wanted to scream that she knew the truth, and that he wasn't fooling her. She wanted to confront him, hit him, kill him. *He's a slime ball!* she thought as she kept her eyes trained ahead. She didn't want to look at him, although she could feel his eyes boring through her. She couldn't stand the feel of his hand in hers. In fact, he disgusted her. But she followed Lander's directions and didn't react. She didn't want Lowell anywhere near her. Skylar wanted to be alone.

When they reached the car, Skylar squeezed between Lowell and Lander as Winnie sat on Lander's other side by the window. It felt so right to feel the warmth of Lander. She knew from his silence on the ride home that he had figured it out. He seemed to be deep in thought. *That's what I need*, thought Skylar, *time to think*.

There was a spontaneous party. Lander was the hero of the day and all of the players and their girls arrived to share in the celebration. John Laverty ordered pizzas and soda to be delivered and music filled the house as the rowdy group rough-housed and celebrated the victory. Skylar stayed with Lowell despite her inner turmoil. It caused a strain and she knew that Lowell was picking up on her feeling. When he kissed her all she could envision was his lips on Winnie. She couldn't respond as she usually did. The affection was all one-sided. Try as she might, Skylar couldn't hide the pain in her eyes. Her heart was wounded. She felt as if her chest would explode with the burning pain that seared her heart.

She saw the quick looks between Winnie and Lowell. They would glance at each other when they thought no one was looking. Winnie had dressed in her tightest jeans, and a sheer see-through blouse. All the players were looking her way, but not with the lust that was in Lowell's eyes. Looking at Lander, Skylar knew that he had noticed. Despite the congratulations and slaps on the back about his touchdown, he seemed remote and serious.

Unaware that they were being watched, Lowell and Winnie found their way to the solarium. In the marble-lined solarium, hanging ferns caught the light of the oversized windows. Potted plants graced the shining marble floors. Behind one of the larger plants, the two lovers found a marble bench. Hidden behind the planter, feeling safe from prying eyes, they indulged their passion. But Lander had followed them, and Skylar was right behind him.

After watching the fervor behind their kisses, Lander finally shouted, "Winnie, I think that we are through!"

Startled, Lander and Winnie separated. Winnie pretended to push Lowell away.

"Oh Lander! I'm so glad that you found me. He was attacking me—forcing himself on me. Thank God you came!" Winnie cried, as she approached Lander and tried to put her arms around him.

Lander stood still. "It didn't look like he was attacking you. From what I saw you were both enjoying yourselves. Well, I say, keep at it. I have no use for someone who can't be faithful."

Winnie's face drained of color as she realized that her cries were not going to save her. Lowell smirked as he rose and approached Lander.

"Oh well!" he laughed. "No use hiding our feelings for each other anymore. Sorry big bro—I guess the better man won!"

Without warning Lander moved quickly and punched Lowell so hard that he fell to the floor. Lander was twice Lowell's size and in his anger did damage. Lowell landed in a sitting position on the white marble floor and held his injured jaw. Unable to speak he sat rubbing the jaw as blood spurted from his lip. Shocked, he didn't have the power to respond. Winnie ran to him, and holding his head close to her breast, screamed.

"You monster! You're nothing but a brute. Lowell told me stories about your abuse and how you always mistreated him. Is it any wonder that I prefer him?" Looking down, Winnie cradled Lowell and stroked his face. "Are you all right?"

Lander seemed shocked by the power of his anger. Turning, he walked away. The rest of the party-goers had heard the shouting and were finding their way into the solarium. Lander disappeared. Skylar watched as Winnie applied ice to Lowell's jaw. He seemed to be basking in the attention.

"I fell and hit my jaw on the ledge." Lowell announced—to the curious stares of the other teenagers.

Another lie, thought Skylar as she watched Winnie fawn over Lowell. She didn't leave, much as she wanted to. She didn't want Winnie and Lowell to see the humiliation in her eyes. Skylar heard the whispers as the girls looked her way to see her reaction. *Dear God—give me the strength I need*, she prayed silently. Skylar remained, sitting in the corner. She felt her heart beating so hard that she thought it might rip right through her chest. She fought back the tears that burned her eyes. It was so painful to sit and watch Winnie gloating over her victory. She waited until the crowd stopped looking at her. She stayed despite her desire to flee, simply because she didn't want to give Winnie the satisfaction of seeing her run.

The pain was unbearable. She felt as if she would melt away if the party lasted much longer. Winnie was the powerful one—the one all the high school girls emulated. Her tall, thin figure and dark flowing hair made her stand out. With flashing dark eyes she ruled the halls of high school. All the girls wanted to be her and all the boys wanted to be with her. Skylar could hardly bear the haughtiness Winnie displayed as she cuddled with Lowell.

Lowell didn't even look Skylar's way. He seemed to revel in the attention of his brother's girl, and the crowd readily accepted Winnie's new choice. Within a few minutes, everyone seemed to forget Skylar. *Maybe I can slip out quietly, without anyone noticing,* she thought. If it didn't end soon she didn't know what she would do. However, without the football hero, the party soon broke up and the last guest, Winnie, left within the hour.

John entered as Winnie left, to help clean up. "Where's the hero? Why did he leave his own party?" he asked looking around.

"Oh, you know Lander. Sometimes he can be so weird. Must have wanted to be alone!" answered Lowell as he stared at Skylar. He seemed to be daring her to tell his father the truth. A look of warning stilled her.

"I don't like it when he disappears," answered John as he finished picking up the last paper plate. "If you know where he is, go get him. I don't like him being out late. It's been a long day."

"How would I know where he is? I don't watch over him," answered Lowell as he headed for his room, "Am I his keeper?"

Skylar headed out the back door. She knew just where Lander was and she knew that he needed her.

Climbing up the ladder to the tree house, she found Lander

sitting slumped against the wall.

"Lander," she whispered as she approached him. She could see that he had been crying heavily, his eyes reddened, his look forlorn.

Looking up at Skylar, he rose and took her in his arms.

"I'm so sorry," she whispered as she held him tight. "I'm so sorry she hurt you."

Pulling her even closer, Lander, with his voice deep and full of pain answered, "It's not Winnie who hurt me. I guess I always sensed that she wasn't who she pretended to be. It's him. How could my own brother betray me?"

Skylar reached up and stroked Lander's moist cheek. "Don't cry! They're not worth it."

Looking down, Lander smiled. "I'm sorry that he hurt you. But maybe he did us both a favor."

Pushing her hair gently back, Lander bent and kissed Skylar, a deep loving kiss. Skylar could feel her heart stop. In that instance all of Skylar's pain disappeared. His warm arms drew her close as his kiss lingered. It felt so right to be in his arms, so right to love him. And she just knew at that moment that she would always love him.

For you formed my inward parts; you knitted me together in my mother's womb. I praise you, for I am fearfully and wonderfully made. Wonderful are your works; my soul knows it very well. My frame was not hidden from you, when I was being made in secret, intricately woven in the depths of the earth. Your eyes saw my unformed substance; in your book were written, every one of them, the days that were formed for me, when as yet there was none of them.
—Psalm 139:13–16

Chapter Fourteen

Secrets: we all have them. We go to great lengths to keep things hidden. We are sure that if others knew our truths they would reject us. So we cover things up, sometimes even lying to ourselves. We can convince ourselves the things we have kept hidden for years don't matter. Perhaps, we dream, they never happened. We push the past down, so deep down that even we can't reach it.

Unfortunately, it always reaches us. The sin we have tried to forget flavors our decisions, our choices, our future. It permeates our very being. We close ourselves off. We even close ourselves off from the only one who can heal us—the only one who can take our past and in forgiving it set us free. We, like Adam and Eve in the garden, hide in naked fear from God.

Winnie turned just in time to catch the look between the two! All night, at the Coles' annual Christmas gala, Lowell had been flirting with the tall blonde in the red dress. Winnie had spent a fortune on her own black cocktail dress, and wore her mother's sparkling diamond necklace. With her black hair swept up with diamond hair pins, she had awed every other male in the room. But while every other male was smitten, Lowell was busy checking out all the other girls.

She wasn't missing the hidden looks that were passing between the blonde and Lowell. It was nothing new. Ever since she had dumped Lander for Lowell, she had been eerily aware that she might have made a mistake. Lowell was constantly looking at and flirting with other girls. He seemed to be bored with her, although she had let him go further than any other boy.

He just pushes and pushes, Winnie thought, aware that he wouldn't be satisfied until she allowed him to sleep with her. *Would that make him faithful?* she wondered as she watched another burning glance between the two. She had her doubts. Lowell turned and smiled at Winnie. Pulling her closer, he whispered in her ear.

"Let's find a spot where we can be alone," he said, his voice deep and suggestive.

Winnie shook her head. "You know how important this party is to my grandfather. I have to stay here and play hostess. He's depending on me to make a good impression."

Lowell smiled but it wasn't convincing. "All right, all right! I'll just go and get us drinks, okay?"

Pulled away by the approach of one of her father's business associates, Winnie lost sight of Lowell. The man was anxious to introduce his second and much younger wife to Winnie. If Winnie accepted her, so would everyone else. Many at the gathering knew and had sympathy for his first wife. The Cole family approval would break the social stigma this crowd held against his former mistress. Knowing the importance of this man's line of distribution to her father's software, Winnie accommodated his need for social recognition. Despite the boring conversation, and the nervous prattling of the young wife, she engaged them in a half-hour talk while the other guests noticed and came to join in the conversation. When she finally walked away they were clearly accepted by the upper-class crowd. Looking around, she couldn't spot Lowell. She couldn't spot the blonde either.

Sighing, she grabbed her coat, and walked through the dazzlingly lit garden to the boat house just beyond the orchard. *Why not,* she thought. *It's where we used to secretly meet.* It didn't take her long to hear the passionate whispers of lovers. Just behind the boat, she spotted them. Stretched out on the cozy couch where she and Lowell used to rendezvous, he was kissing the blonde in the red dress.

Winnie held back. She wasn't surprised. She didn't confront them. The blonde was the state senator's underage daughter. Winnie smiled. She didn't have strong feelings for Lowell. Not like what she had felt for Lander. *How can I work this to my advantage?* She took out her phone and snapped a picture of the two on the couch. *This could work,* she thought as she quietly slipped away. Returning to the party, she felt her mood lighten. Lowell would pay for his indiscretion. Just not in the way he expected.

*

"It's none of your business!" John shouted, standing up. Bridget entered the room quietly as John raised his voice. There was a slight smile on her face. The others barely noticed her, so used to her silent presence. Regina reddened with anger at his resistance. *I will break those two up,* she thought as she envisioned Lander and Skylar together. It had been going on for months. At first, she had thought that it would burn itself out. *How could a simpering nobody like Skylar keep his interest?* she had thought. But now the romance was not only flourishing, but seemed to be growing stronger. The two were inseparable—together all the time. Holding hands and cooing up in each other's face. Regina was not going to permit it.

"I have plans for Lander," she announced, "and none of those plans include that girl. I told you to get rid of her in the beginning. She is not in the same class as Lander and she will only bring him down."

John exhaled slowly through his mouth. Closing the door to the study, he hoped that Skylar couldn't hear the argument.

"I think that they make a great couple. Besides, they are just teenagers and I won't allow you to interfere with their relationship,"

John answered, as he swept his hand through his hair.

Walking past Bridget who sat in the corner chair, John raised his finger and shouted, "Regina, I swear, if you cause trouble I'll never forget it. I want you to drop this whole subject."

Regina resisted the urge to claw him. *Who the hell does he think he is?* she thought as her eyes narrowed. He stood tall before her, not backing down. Looking past him, Regina could see Bridget watching.

"You kept that girl despite what it did to my daughter! Didn't you think of her when you decided to raise that whore's offspring? I won't let her have Lander. She's nobody—without a father's name! Why should she take this family's name?" Regina spit all her venom directly at her son-in-law.

"Skylar is my daughter! I raised her and she is a wonderfully sweet, caring girl. As far as I'm concerned Lander couldn't do any better," John snarled through clenched teeth.

"Ha! What can she do for him? She has no grace, nor can she learn it. You have to be born with it. Winnie Cole, now there's a girl that can help him get ahead in the world. A woman with her breeding can help him reach the pinnacle in any business," Regina hissed.

John's jaw tightened. "That's enough! You will not meddle with Lander and Skylar. They're young and time alone will tell how their relationship will develop. I won't allow you to push your way in."

Bridget rose, and stood beside her husband, wrapping her arm in his. *I'm so proud of him,* she thought as he seemed to stand taller with his wife beside him.

Regina snarled sarcastically, "So you stand by your man."

Bridget smiled and reaching for the right word answered, "Yes!"

It had been a struggle to learn how to draw the words she needed from deep inside. Ever since the football game, she had found the courage to try. Through a slow process of trial and error, Bridget had started to communicate. With the help of her husband and the speech coaches he hired she practiced daily. It was starting to show. She didn't join in long drawn-out conversations, but she could answer simple questions and engage in social settings.

However, most of her words were saved for her husband. *I can finally tell him that I love him,* Bridget thought, as she stood firmly at his side. *Together we can stand up to my mother.* She was so proud of the changes the years had brought to John. Still handsome with a touch of gray in his hair, he had grown enough backbone to earn her respect. And in sharing a renewed love they had found the joy that the years had robbed. *Soon it will be time,* Bridget thought. *Time to carve out a new life.*

*

John had closed the door to muffle the sounds of raised voices, but it was too late. Skylar sat on the staircase landing, the same landing that Lowell and she used to frequent as children—children who always felt excluded and separated from the "crown prince," as Lowell liked to call him.

Now I'm in love with the crown prince, Skylar thought as tears formed in her eyes. Skylar knew the power of this woman. Regina had great influence and John had never proved much of a match. In the past, she had crushed him like a steam roller. The only time that he had successfully stood up to Regina was when he decided that he would raise her. *Did he win the battle, or is this just a continuation?* Skylar thought as she listened to the ongoing quarrel.

Why was she calling her mother a whore? Skylar wondered. Was there something she didn't know? She had always been curious about her own family. Once, when she was just ten, she and Lowell tried to solve the mystery of her roots. They had snuck into the files in John's home office. Hoping to find some information, they hadn't been disappointed. They found papers that had the address her mother had given on her application—her family address.

Lowell and Skylar had written the address down and taken the bus to the neighborhood. Like in the Nancy Drew mysteries Skylar loved to read, they had staked out the house from across the street. It was deadly quiet, and after an hour they were bored and decided to leave. That's when the front door opened and a young man stood in the doorway with an older man and woman. The young man kissed both, and was apparently leaving after a visit. Lowell wanted to go up to the door and knock, but Skylar could feel the knot in her stomach growing.

"Let's go home. I don't feel so well," she had told him.

"You do look pale," Lowell answered as they walked the two blocks to the bus stop. "Maybe we can come back another time."

"Sure," answered Skylar as she held her stomach. But they never did. The subject was dropped and she never felt the draw to uncover her past again.

Now I need to know! she decided as she rose from her hiding place on the staircase. Skylar had kept the address written in childlike scribbles in her wallet over the years. With each new purse and wallet, she had tucked the worn paper in hidden crevices. *Someday I may need this,* she thought with each transfer. But she never returned to the house on the other side of town. It wasn't something she felt prepared to do. All she knew was that her mother gave her life to save her, and that seemed enough.

Enough until now, she resolved as she put on her jacket and headed to the nearest bus stop. *Now I need to know.* Her hands grew cold and clammy as she rode the bus across town. She noticed that her stomach was churning as she walked the few blocks to the neighborhood of neat Cape Cods. Skylar was surprised how much her hands shook as she reached for the doorbell.

The old man just stared as he opened the front door. "Yes, may I help you?"

Skylar choked, unable to speak. She found herself staring into her own brown eyes.

"Yes?" the man asked again, seeming exasperated.

She nervously smiled. "I think I may be your granddaughter!"

"Vera!" the man called to someone behind him. "Come here!"

An older woman appeared quickly and stared at the intruder.

"This girl claims that she is our granddaughter," the older man announced.

"You're nobody to us—just like your mother was nothing to us!" the woman croaked. "Better be on your way."

Skylar was shocked. "Aren't you going to ask me in?"

"What is it you want? Money?" asked the man.

"No…no," Skylar stammered. "I would just like to learn something about my mother."

"Well, here you are," answered the older man in a sarcastic voice. "Your mother had you without benefit of marriage and we disowned her and you years ago. Now be on your way! There's no one here for you!"

The door slammed so forcefully that it almost hit Skylar in the face.

*

"Vera, you better call Mrs. Kagan and let her know the girl has been here," he announced as he turned away from the door. The older woman headed to the phone. She hadn't spoken to Mrs. Kagan since she had stopped by after Hannah's funeral.

The wealthy woman had offered them money to take Skylar and raise her, but they had refused. They hadn't refused the large amount she offered when her son-in-law had applied to adopt Skylar. As per her instructions, they had put in an objection and demanded that Skylar be returned to their family. As soon as John withdrew his request to adopt the girl, they had renounced their demand for her return. It had happened twice and both times they had received a large check from Regina. Picking up the phone, Vera dialed the number she had been given. She knew where her loyalty lied.

*

Shaken, Skylar returned to the bus stop without thought. Staring out the window, she paled as her stomach cramped. *They don't want me,* she mused. *No one wants me. My own grandparents apparently didn't want me!*

She got off the bus before the stop that would bring her home. Walking three blocks down the side road, she entered the cemetery under the arch that read St. Joseph's. It had been a year since her last visit, but she found the site easily. Her father or the man she thought of as her father, had placed a beautiful granite stone on her mother's grave. Carved in the stone was a winding rosary. The last time they had brought flowers—on mother's day—he had told Skylar how often he had seen her mother praying the rosary. *If only I could talk to her now,* cried the young girl as she fell to her knees on her mother's grave. Skylar wept, letting all the pain and the sense of rejection fall as tears on Hannah's grave. When she was all cried out she walked away, unaware that her mother had listened, not knowing her angel held her.

Arriving home, Skylar felt numb. Looking at the house where the residents had just argued about her, she knew that she couldn't go in. She went to the garden, which was now bare and brown because of the cold winds of winter. She sat on the deck that she used to share with her mother. She had only hazy memories of Hannah: warm hands and smiles were woven deeply into her mind. Skylar didn't know if they were actual memories or just imaginings from the few stories she had heard.

It doesn't matter, she thought as tears began to fall. *No one wants me now.* The numb feeling wore off—the emotions erupted. Alone in the cottage garden, Skylar wept again. She didn't hear the garden gate open. She didn't hear the footsteps. She only knew that his arms were around her once more, warming her cold spirit as she told him her sad tale. Sobbing deeply, she let all of the pain of her past rise to the surface. As a child, she had always felt the coldness of Regina. It had made her hide in corners or on staircases, watching a life in which she never felt a part. The one relationship that kept her hopeful was the close friendship she had shared with Lowell. Now that he was too busy with his new love, Winnie, she felt completely unwanted. Rejection by his grandmother and rejection by her natural family had broken her heart.

Lander held her close. He allowed her to cry out her pain. He waited patiently until the tears ran dry. As the sobs became gentle, he reached underneath and raised her face to him by lifting her chin. Looking into his eyes she could see the warm love that she craved. She wanted to fall into those eyes, that bottomless love.

"You don't need them," he whispered. "You have me." Slipping his class ring off his finger, he placed it on her slender ring finger.

"Will you be my girl?" he asked with a smile.

"But what about your grandmother? I just told you what she said," she cried.

"Granny? Don't worry. I'll take care of her," He smiled.

Skylar could feel her heart soar, "Yes, yes!"

"And as my girl, naturally, you would go to the prom with me?" he smiled as he kissed her cheek and wiped away her tears.

"Yes," was all she could say.

For now we see in a mirror dimly, but then face to face. Now I know in part; then I shall know fully, even as I have been fully known.
— 1 Corinthians 13:12

Chapter Fifteen

Insecurities eat away at the truth. We see life through the prism of our wounded hearts and the view is distorted. It is like looking through beveled glass. Some things look larger than they are, while the larger images can disappear into a blur of color.

There is only one way to see truth. That is to know who we truly are. When we know who we are, the lies of this world cannot bend and distort the light. We can see the truth only when we look through the clear glass of Love. It all comes into focus when we see everything through the light of Christ.

Skylar felt as if she were living a dream. Each morning Lander would meet her at the breakfast table and drive her to school. All during the day, the football hero would meet her in the hall, or at her locker. And every time she saw him, she could feel her heart stop. His green eyes sparkled each time he looked at her. She could see his muscles ripple beneath his shirt. When he walked into a room, everyone noticed. He had a presence and she was stunned to be standing at his side, his girl. *How could he love me?* she wondered. However, when Skylar was with him—held in his arms—there was no question how he felt.

She felt as if she finally belonged to someone. She could feel the cold glances from the other girls in school. *They're just jealous,* she thought as she proudly held his hand walking down the hall. The haughty looks she got from Regina were another matter. Those were threatening. She decided to ignore the older woman. Skylar decided to trust in her own happiness. Lander loved her. She was sure of his feelings. She felt safe. She was confident that he would protect her.

It surprised Skylar when Bridget knocked on her door that Saturday morning. It was just a few months until the prom and she had been planning a trip to the mall to look at gowns.

"Can I come in?" Bridget asked softly.

Knowing how hard it was for Bridget to speak, Skylar opened her door and showed her to a chair.

In halting speech, Bridget asked, "Have you found a dress?"

"No, I was going to start shopping today," she answered, "but I'm a little nervous about picking the right one."

"May..." Bridget hesitated, "May... I go with you?"

Skylar was stunned. She never had a mother to help her shop or teach her how to dress. Bridget had always been like a ghost in her life, a presence that shadowed the corners, a woman who was always in the background and one Skylar barely noticed. Regina, the only other woman in her life, hated her. When Skylar saw other girls shopping with their mothers, she had really missed her own. Now Bridget, who had grown up educated in style and grace, wanted to help her. *I can't believe it,* she smiled.

"Of course," Skylar answered as she took both of Bridget's hands in hers. "I need all the help I can get. I want to look perfect for Lander, and I've never shopped for such an important dress."

Dress after dress seemed so wrong. Skylar could feel the tears forming as she once again paraded out of the dressing room. She had put on yet another dress which had looked so wonderful on the hanger, but looked horrible on her. It was her fifteenth dress and she was ready to give up. Bridget sat on a chair in front of the mirrored platform, shaking her head negatively with each presentation.

Skylar's heart sank as she watched a girl at the next station stunningly show a dress she had already tried on. *Maybe it's not the dresses. Maybe it's me,* she thought as Bridget again shook her head in disapproval. The dress she was now wearing had a princess bodice covered with sequins. It flowed out from the waist in layers of chiffon. It looked horrible. Skylar could feel her heart ache. She wanted to please Lander but she was now convinced that no matter what she would look terrible.

Bridget left her chair and came back with a white dress. It was so plain. It had an empire waist defined by a blue sash. It was mermaid style—it was cut close to the body, and the simple silk was covered with a lace overlay. It didn't sparkle or shine with flashy colors like the other dresses she had tried on. It wasn't what Skylar imagined a prom dress to look like.

Taking the dress, Skylar nodded. *I'll try this on but I hate it,* she thought as she hung it on the hook. It was much too plain, but she didn't want to hurt Bridget's feelings. Slipping it on, and zipping the back, Skylar was shocked when she stepped out of the dressing room and looked in the mirror. She looked great! Her petite figure was accentuated by the easy style. She didn't look lost as she did in all the layered gowns. Looking down, Skylar could see Bridget nodding and smiling. The dress was perfect for her. They added simple strappy white shoes with kitten heels to complete the look.

"You're too tiny for those large gowns. You're so pretty that they take away from you. Always remember—simple!" Bridget instructed slowly, looking for the right words.

Skylar was in heaven. Hanging the new gown on her closet door, she stared at it each night before she slept. She dreamt of Lander's face when he saw her wearing it. Everything was perfect.

*

Lander was surprised to find Winnie sitting in his grandmother's office. *What could this be about?* he wondered. He took a seat next to Winnie facing Regina's desk. Secretly, he had hoped the meeting Granny called was just about business. He had received a full scholarship from his second choice college. Within a few weeks he would be graduating and after the summer, he would be heading across country to study medicine. He knew that his grandmother wanted him to get a business degree and he didn't have the heart to tell her that he had decided to be a doctor. Perhaps, she was trying to push him ahead with a summer job in the Coles' company. He had already turned down an internship at the Kagan Corp. If she kept pushing, he would have to tell her about his pre-med. major before he had planned to. Lander had been praying for a quiet summer.

"I called you here to ask you to change your plans for the prom," Regina surprised him.

"What do you mean?" Lander asked quizzically.

"I want you to take Winnie as your date. And before you answer, let me tell you why," she continued.

Lander couldn't believe his ears, but he decided to hear her out.

"I know you made plans to take Skylar, but I think that under the circumstances you might want to change your plans. The Coles, and especially Winnie, have been close to this family for years." Regina nodded at Winnie, who took out a Kleenex and dabbed her eyes.

"What do you mean? I am bringing Skylar!" Lander insisted. "Why doesn't Winnie go with Lowell? They've been dating for almost a year."

Winnie sobbed, "I can't go with him! I found him with another girl."

"Your brother is no good. He never was!" insisted Regina.

"I paid a thousand for my dress, only to discover that he was cheating on me! Now what am I going to tell my family and friends?" asked Winnie.

"Skylar has a dress also! How can I disappoint her?" Lander asked.

"Skylar will understand. Besides, I'm not saying that Skylar shouldn't go to the prom. I just want you to escort Winnie as your date. Take her there just to save face. Just a few dances and as beautiful as she is Winnie will find plenty of boys to dance with. It's just for show. You can spend most of the night with little Skylar if you wish," announced Regina firmly.

Lander was floored. "I can't do that to Skylar. She's been looking forward to the prom for months."

"Oh..." Winnie sobbed into the tissue. "I'll never be able to show my face again—and to miss my prom!"

"Skylar is not even a senior. It isn't her prom. This is Winnie's senior prom—her only prom. You can take Skylar to her own senior prom when it comes up. But poor Winnie will never get another chance. Don't be selfish!" said Regina.

Lander rose to his feet, and brushing his hand through his hair, paced around the room. "I can't disappoint Skylar. Couldn't you make it up with Lowell? Couldn't you just pretend to like him for one night?"

"No," cried Winnie. "I can't stand to have him touch me!" Pulling out her phone, she touched the screen until she reached the photo. "See your brother! See how low he has sunk!"

Looking at the phone, Lander stepped back in shock. "Why she's just a fourteen year old girl!"

"So you understand," cooed Winnie. "You'll be my date—I can't go with Lowell."

"But what about Skylar?" answered Lander, looking back and forth from his grandmother to Winnie.

Regina smiled. *We've won! Now it's just a matter of logistics.*

"Skylar can still go to the prom. Lowell can take her," Regina announced.

Lander turned to his grandmother with a look of shock.

"Oh, don't be silly!" laughed Regina. "Lowell and Skylar have been friends all their life. He wouldn't harm her. Besides, it's just for the arrival. You couldn't be so cruel as to leave Winnie hanging. You can all go in the same limo and once the fact that you escorted Winnie is established you can spend your night with Skylar."

Turning to Winnie, Regina smiled. "There now, dear! It's all settled. I knew Lander wouldn't let us down."

*

Skylar was devastated. She could feel her heart breaking as he explained Winnie's dilemma. Lander didn't go into detail. He didn't want to spread Lowell's bad behavior around.

"It's just for show," Lander repeated his grandmother's words. "It's just for Winnie's prom!"

Skylar couldn't breathe. Her dreams were crashing down around her. She wanted to believe that Lander was just trying to be kind to an old friend.

He still loves her! Skylar's heart cried. *I've never been good enough!* Her chest burnt from pushing the tears down. Skylar couldn't bear the pain. She sat in silent torture, as she watched everything she had hoped for disappearing before her eyes.

Lander mistook her silence for understanding. "You're a wonderful girl—and I love you!"

She heard him, but she didn't believe him. Skylar knew now that she would never be good enough for Lander. *Lowell was always right. Lander is the crown prince and I am the illegitimate daughter of a servant.*

"So Lowell will take me?" Skylar asked.

"Yes, yes…" Lander smiled. "It will be a wonderful night. You and I will be together once Winnie mixes with others. Don't worry, everything will be fine."

The night of the prom, Bridget fixed Skylar's hair. Sweeping it up in a French twist, she allowed loose tendrils of blonde curls down to frame Skylar's oval face. She placed small flowers throughout her hair. With make-up carefully applied, Skylar's brown eyes glowed and her creamy complexion stood out. Skylar was shocked when she looked in the mirror. She had never thought she could look this way. Skylar glowed with the look of a princess.

Stoic, she steeled herself to face the night ahead. She didn't want to see Lander with Winnie. She didn't know how she was going to stand silently by as he danced with Winnie. Skylar smiled as she descended the stairs. Lander and Lowell stood at the bottom of the staircase. She tried not to look at either of them. Bridget and John were there taking pictures. Skylar tried to keep her eyes on the only parents she had ever known. Unable to help herself, she glanced at Lander. His eyes were full of love. He seemed to be seeing her for the first time.

Skylar turned away. She knew better. *I won't lie to myself any more. It's Winnie he is taking to the prom.* Turning she looked at Lowell. What she saw in his eyes was completely different. He seemed to be devouring her with his eyes. It startled her. However, as she reached the bottom of the stairs, she placed her hand in Lowell's. Lander looked a little surprised, standing back and staring at the couple as pictures were being taken. Skylar smiled at Lowell. He was her date after all.

Winnie swept into the limo like a queen. Her red silk dress accented her dark hair and eyes, giving her the look of a tall wild gypsy. She had insisted on a red dress for a reason and looking at Lowell's response she knew she had hit her mark. Thousands of sequins sparkled on the low-cut bodice. The two girls couldn't look more opposite.

Winnie, sitting next to Lander, held his arm and his attention for the duration of the ride. Skylar tried to ignore the playful touches and sultry whispers. Lowell was sitting much too close. She felt hot and uncomfortable.

Leaning over, he whispered in Skylar's ear, "You're gorgeous!"

Skylar wanted to scream as she and Lowell walked into the dance behind Winnie and Lander. She held Lowell's arm more for support than for show. *How am I going to get through this night?* she wondered. *Will Lander really leave Winnie and come to me?* her heart cried.

*

Winnie glanced behind at Skylar. She could read the pain that Skylar was feeling on her face. *I have to admit,* Winnie mused, *she really looks beautiful.* She wasn't worried. Her plan was working perfectly. It had been months in the making. She had lain awake nights, ever since she had caught Lowell with that girl. She had gone over every contingency in her mind. It was a foolproof plan. She knew it would work because she had studied all of them. She knew all the players. And that knowledge would get her exactly what she wanted.

Winnie wanted Lander back. It was as simple as that. And if she had to use a little blackmail to get what she wanted it didn't bother her in the least. Lowell had been shocked when she confronted him. He had thought he had gotten away with it. Winnie had waited. A threat was only good when it was fresh on the mind. She didn't want to give Lowell too much time to figure a way out of his situation.

"You wouldn't post that on the internet?" he had asked, knowing full well that she would.

"I won't if you do exactly as I say!" she had insisted.

Dancing the first dance with Lander, she held her body close to him. She wanted to entice him. She could see him glancing over to Skylar and Lowell as they danced. *Look all you want to*, she thought. *Soon you will be back with me and Skylar will want nothing to do with you.*

After a few dances, Lander seemed anxious to break away. Taking his arm, Winnie guided him to the balcony. Soft lights glimmered above the railing and lent a romantic glow to the deserted spot.

"What do you want?" Lander asked.

"I just wanted to be alone. I just want to thank you for helping me out tonight," Winnie smiled as she put her arms around him. "Can't I give you a little thank you kiss?"

Putting her hands behind his neck, Winnie pulled him down to her. Holding him tightly she gave him a long passionate kiss.

Lander pulled away. "What are you doing?"

Winnie smiled. Lander hadn't heard Lowell guide Skylar to the balcony. He didn't hear her gasp. He didn't hear her run with Lowell in hot pursuit.

"Lander, Lander! Don't you realize that we belong together?" Winnie laughed as he left to find Skylar. Winnie wasn't worried. Her plan was in motion.

For freedom Christ has set us free; stand firm therefore, and do not submit again to a yoke of slavery.
—Galatians 5:1

Chapter Sixteen

We aren't given rules to keep us enslaved. He gives us rules to keep us free, free to live our best life. God knows our nature. He created it. He wants us to have free will—to be able to live our dreams. The rules are to protect us from losing our freedom. The devil shouts about freedom, doing things our own way—without God. We rebel, thinking we are asserting our rights. But it is sin that ensnares. It is sin that traps.

Skylar didn't know where she was going. She just knew that she had to get away. The image of Lander's and Winnie's passionate kiss was seared in her mind. It mocked her as she tried to argue with it. It belittled her belief in love, the once in a lifetime love she thought she shared with Lander. She ran across the dance floor unaware of the stares of others. She turned down the first hallway past the banquet room. The halls became darker as she got closer to the kitchen.

The sounds of clanging pots and the buzz of activity coming from the kitchen pushed her on. Skylar shivered at the thought of seeing others. Praying that no one would come out of the kitchen, she ran. She only knew that she had to get away. *There has to be a back door out of here!* her mind screamed as she hit a dead end. Turning back she spotted a side hall. Skylar ran, but she was losing her breath. Her heart had been pounding since she had seen Lander in Winnie's arms. Tears blurred her vision. Skylar stumbled and would have fallen if he hadn't caught her.

"Come with me," he whispered as she allowed him to guide her. Pushing open a door, Lowell led her into a small lounge. She heard the lock click, but it didn't register. She was in too much pain. Lowell led her to a padded bench that lined the small room and sitting down took her in his arms.

"Sh...." he whispered as he held her close "You must have known that you couldn't really trust him. Don't you remember what it was like growing up with him?"

Skylar clung to Lowell. She needed a safe place, a familiar place, "How could he do that to me? How could I be so stupid?"

Brushing her hair from her face, he continued, "It's always been us. It's always been about us."

Skylar couldn't understand what he was saying. Her pain was too loud. She thought her heart was going to burst through her chest. His arms were comforting, his warmth inviting.

His lips brushed across her cheek, reaching for her mouth. Finding her lips, he kissed her lightly, then deeply. She didn't pull away. It felt safe, warm. She wanted to be loved. All her life she wanted to be loved. And who had been there, right beside her, wanting that same love? They understood each other. Sharing long childhood days, and lonely nights, they had shared a lifetime of pain.

And here he is again, Skylar thought, as he lowered her to the bench. She could feel his warm lips on her throat, and then his kisses returned to her lips.

Suddenly the image of Lander kissing Winnie returned, and she pulled away. *What am I doing?* She pushed Lowell away. *This isn't right- I love Lander,* she remembered.

"No...stop!" she mumbled as she stood up.

She could feel his anger. His face flushed with passion a minute ago now looked annoyed.

He stood and wrapped his arms around her. Pulling her closer Lowell pressed himself against her.

"No...I still love him," she wept.

Lowell pulled back and stood apart. "Him! How can you love him? After what he's done to you? After what he's done to all of us?"

Skylar took a deep breath. She felt confused, her mind fuzzy.

"I have to talk to him. I have to find if he loves her. I have to find out the truth," she answered.

Skylar walked to the door and tried unsuccessfully to open the latch. She could feel Lowell behind her. Reaching around he pulled her away from the door and turned her to face him.

"Why would you want to talk to him, the crown prince? He was only playing with you. He was always slated to be with Winnie Cole. Two companies merging in marriage. You and I never had a chance. Don't you remember?" Lowell whispered as he slowly led her back to the bench.

Skylar sighed. Lowell was right. They had always been the outsiders. All through their lonely childhood they had clung to each other. Whenever one of them was spurned or hurt by others, they found safety in their friendship. *I need to be loved. Why pine for a love I can never have? Why not take the love that is offered?*

Skylar allowed him to cover her with kisses. She allowed Lowell to unzip her dress. Her mind was numb. She felt as if her soul had died. She needed his warmth, his passion to come back to life.

Without any further resistance, she melted. Without the love she wanted, Skylar settled for the love at hand.

*

She didn't remember dozing off. The morning light was still slightly gray, still clinging to the fading night. Skylar didn't recall where she was at first. She could feel his warm body next to her and sitting up was shocked to see his black hair lying on the pillow he had created from her prom dress.

Oh my Lord! her mind cried as the memories of the previous night were awakened. *What have I done?* Her heart jumped as Lowell rolled over and opened his eyes.

"Good morning, Baby," he murmured as he sat up beside her.

"What happened?" Skylar asked, knowing instantly what a stupid question it was. It was obvious what had happened.

Lowell smiled and reaching over pulled her to him. After a long passionate kiss, he pulled back and grinned again.

"Heaven happened. Don't you remember?" he laughed as he rose and started to dress.

Flushed with embarrassment, Skylar wished that she didn't remember. She remembered coming here with Lowell. She remembered how he had comforted her. She remembered the passion that followed. But worse, she remembered what caused the entire episode. *Lander, Lander and Winnie,* she could feel her heart ache as the image rose.

"We better get home," Lowell said as he donned his jacket. "It's almost morning and we should try to get to our rooms before they notice we're missing."

Fear gripped Skylar as she thought of others knowing what she had done. Dressing quickly, she tried to arrange her disheveled hair with the small comb in her evening purse. It was no use. She looked so different from how she looked last evening. She had looked so fresh, so lovely. *Now, I just look a mess. Oh God, I'm so sorry.* Thinking of Lander and the way he had looked at her as she descended the staircase made her heart ache. *What would he think if he could see me now?* she thought.

During the day it was easy to navigate the halls that had seemed so mysterious the night before. Everything looked different in the light of day. Lowell led her, holding her hand, to the back door and out to the nearest bus stop. The bus was loaded with commuters on their way to work. Skylar could see them looking at her. With Lowell in his tux and her in her gown, the commuters had to know that they had spent the night together. Skylar couldn't look at the people—she stared out the window the whole trip. She just wanted to get home. She wanted to shower, a hot shower to wash away her sin.

Walking down the drive, she could see the sun rising behind the Kagan mansion. Lowell pulled her to him and holding her close kissed her before he opened the front door. Skylar felt numb. She needed to be alone. She needed to think about what had happened.

As Lowell put his key in the door, he turned to her and said, "Don't worry. They are probably all still in bed. If we're quiet they will never know how late we got home."

Skylar prayed that he was right. She couldn't imagine the shame of tumbling in at this hour. *If only I can wash. Get these clothes off,* she thought. Skylar wanted to forget last night and all that had happened. If she could forget, her unconscious mind whispered, maybe it wouldn't matter. Maybe it could be like it never happened. She kept that hope for just a minute, a fleeting moment. It disappeared when the front door opened.

"Here they are!" shouted John. "We were just about to call the police. Where were you all night?"

John and Bridget were standing in the foyer. They were dressed in robes and slippers, and it was clear that they had been up all night. Skylar knew how wrinkled her beautiful gown was; she could see Bridget staring at it. She was so embarrassed. It was horrible meeting John and Bridget this way. The last thing Skylar ever wanted to do was disappoint them. However, the worst was seeing Lander standing there. He looked relieved for just a moment, relieved to see her safe. However, he didn't come to her. He didn't reach for her. She could see it in his eyes. The instant sense of relief at her safety passed quickly. He kept his face emotionless, but his eyes couldn't hide his feelings.

"Sorry, sorry," Lowell held up his hands. "We spent some time talking—late into the night. Then we just fell asleep. Didn't mean to worry you," he said with a casual lilt.

"So long as both of you are safe!" answered John. "We were up all night. When Lander came home so early we knew something was wrong. He and the limo driver searched for you but couldn't find you. He thought he would find you when he got home."

Bridget added, "When you didn't come home, we worried that maybe you fell in with the wrong crowd—maybe taken a ride with someone who had been drinking."

"No, just fell asleep. Sorry to worry you," Lowell answered, grinning at Lander.

Skylar remained silent. She couldn't look at Lander. She felt so ashamed. Lander was silent as he looked from Lowell to Skylar. She could feel his gaze burning through her. *He knows!* her mind screamed as she blushed. *He knows what I did.* She didn't believe her heart could hurt worse than it did last night. Looking up, she could see the pain in his eyes.

She followed his gaze. Looking down, she could see Lowell's dark hair. Strains of dark hair were all over the front of her white dress. She could see Bridget and Lander staring at the wrinkled, sullied gown. *The white gown that Bridget had helped her pick out, the gown so white and pure,* her mind screamed. The gown Lowell had used for a pillow. Skylar couldn't bear it.

Running up the stairs, she could feel her tears starting. In her room she stripped the gown off and kicked it under the bed. The gown she had dreamt of, the gown she had hung on her closet door now seemed a dirty rag. Skylar almost burned herself with the hot water in the shower. Taking a soapy sponge, she scrubbed her skin repeatedly until it felt raw. Donning a cotton nightgown, she stumbled into bed. *It's no use!* she wept, *I can't scrub the sin away.*

Skylar was unable to get the sight of Lander's disappointment out of her mind and found it impossible to rest. She stayed hidden in bed. She wasn't ready to see anyone. She couldn't look any of them in the eye. *Lander knows,* her heart cried. She knew that it was over now. He would never forgive her. They would never be together again. *Why was he kissing Winnie? Why?* Her mind was fevered with emotion. Maybe Lowell was right. It was always about Winnie and Lander. Maybe nothing was different. Maybe she did belong with Lowell.

However, as she fell into a light restless sleep, her dreams were of Lander. In her dream she was dressed in the white prom gown. Holding a bouquet of white roses, she was walking up the church aisle holding John Laverty's arm. He was going to give her away in marriage. Music played as she walked slowly up the aisle to the man she loved. She could see his back—he was waiting, waiting to share his life with her. It was difficult to see through the netting of her veil. When she reached the altar, John stood beside her and the groom turned and lifted the front of her veil. Skylar reached for her groom. She reached for Lander. But when she saw the groom it was Lowell.

Shocked, Skylar turned to look at the people in the church. There was Winnie! She was clinging to Lander and they were both laughing. Turning away, Skylar could see that everyone in the church was laughing. They all knew—everyone knew! Turning again she could see that Lowell was laughing too! She was trapped.

Skylar awoke in a cold sweat. *It's hopeless. What am I going to do?* She opened the nightstand next to her bed and rummaged through the top drawer. She pulled out the case she had been searching for. Unzipping the tiny case, she pulled the set of rosaries out, Hannah's rosary beads. Getting down on her knees beside the bed, Skylar cried, "Blessed Mother help me!" Holding the beads and bowing her head she started. "I believe in God…."

No temptation has overtaken you that is not common to man. God is faithful, and he will not let you be tempted beyond your ability, but with the temptation he will also provide the way of escape, that you may be able to endure it.
— 1 Corinthians 10:13

Chapter Seventeen

Sins are constant, little offenses that nibble at our soul. But youth carries the burden. A burden that weighs us down, judges us. It ends our childhood, that magical time of unlimited possibilities. For with the knowledge of evil, the evil that we carry in ourselves, we are tossed from Eden. Knowing who we are and what we are capable of, we enter the cold. We hide in the outside world. Naked and exposed, we think we are alone.

Lowell walked around the upper offices of Anthony Cole's company. *Someday this will be mine,* he thought as the woman who was doing the orientation droned on. He had taken the summer job that Lander had refused. He was a little irritated that, once again, he was taking Lander's leavings, but he swallowed his pride. *It will work out in the end,* he thought. One of the older workers gave him—the newbie—the order for everyone's coffee. The middle-aged and slightly balding manager seemed to be enjoying the power to push him around. *Enjoy yourself now, buddy,* Lowell mused, making a mental note of the man's name.

Lowell had forced Winnie into talking to her father. The offer for the job came the next day. It was partial payment for his part in the prom night fiasco. The rest of her payment was the deletion of the photo she had on her iphone. He wasn't angry about it. In fact, he admired her ingenuity. He had profited from her devious manipulation. Lowell had enjoyed his night with Skylar, even though his attempts to have another had been spurned. It gave him great pleasure to see the pain that the crown prince suffered over the incident. *A crown prince about to lose his throne!* he laughed as he headed out to get the crowd their java.

Spotting Winnie waiting outside her father's office, he stopped. She looked luscious in her yellow sundress.

"Hey Sweetheart—what's happening?" Lowell asked as he sat down beside her.

Clearly unhappy, she gave him a withering look. "You look happy. I guess you've gotten everything that you wanted."

Lowell laughed. He knew what she was referring to. Winnie's plan to win Lander's affection had back-fired. Lander wanted nothing to do with her. In fact, he seemed to blame her for everything that had happened. It had been weeks and while Lander wasn't seeing Skylar any more, he wasn't courting Winnie, either. *He's a fool!* thought Lowell as he looked at the tall brunette. N*ot only is she hot, she's rich.*

"So what are you doing here? Need some money from the old man?" Lowell laughed.

"I wish. Daddy got this stupid idea that I should have a job this summer. He thinks I should learn the workings of the company before I go away to college," she pouted.

"It won't be so bad! Maybe we could find some time alone," Lowell whispered as he leaned over to nibble her ear.

"Maybe." She pulled away.

Just then the knob on the office door twisted, and Lowell scrambled to get out of sight. *No sense getting caught fooling around the first day,* he thought. Lowell was glad when the day ended and he could head home for dinner.

Family dinners had been pretty dreadful since prom night. The silence between Lander and Skylar hung over the table like a black cloud. Bridget had insisted that everyone share at least one meal a day. Lowell figured it was her way of trying to get Lander and Skylar back together and so far it wasn't working. Even Regina joined the family. *She's enjoying the break-up,* thought Lowell. He knew her plans for Lander. Lowell had known her big plans all his life. The crown prince, heir to the company, was supposed to marry Winnie and create the merger that would make Kagan Inc. the largest publishing and software company in the world. *Oh well,* Lowell thought, *"the best laid plans of mice and men…"*

Lowell observed the little glances that Lander cast Skylar's way. *He's still in love with her,* he realized with amusement. Skylar, clearly sure that Lander was through with her, didn't seem to notice. She sat across from Bridget and the two talked female nonsense all night. Regina had noticed the distance between Lander and Skylar. Lowell saw the smirk on the old lady's face. He hated the bitch! Watching the dynamics gave Lowell an idea. The one way he could cement his plans was to get Lander and Skylar back together. *Not only will it clear a path for me,* he decided, *it just might kill the old lady!*

It didn't prove hard. While both their cell phones were charging in the hall, he sent a text to Skylar from Lander's phone—insisting that she meet him in the cottage garden that night. Lowell sent the same text to Lander from Skylar's cell. *There's fire between those two, and it won't take much to make it spark*, he thought.

*

Lander was shocked when he read the message from Skylar. She had been ignoring him for weeks. He knew that she had seen him kissing Winnie. *Winnie! I'd like to wring her neck!* he thought. She hadn't come home that night and it was clear that something had happened between her and Lowell. It killed him to see her each day. He wanted to reach out and hug her. He could see the pain on her face and knew that she would never trust him again. How could he blame her? She was so fragile, so insecure, and his behavior had been her worse nightmare.

Why did I listen to Granny? I know that she's always wanted me to be with Winnie, he grimaced. *How stupid could I be?* Seeing the pain in Skylar's eyes had been more then he could bear. Now she was reaching out to him and he hoped she would forgive him. Thinking of Lowell—he hoped that Skylar would end his doubts, his horrid suspicions.

*

Skylar was upset when she got the text. She was afraid. Maybe he just wants to tell me that we are finally through—that he knows I slept with Lowell. Still, her heart leapt with hope. *I still love him, even though he betrayed me,* she realized.

How can I ever trust him again? He always goes back to Winnie. Winnie has everything. She's popular, beautiful, and socially acceptable. I'm just the little illegitimate daughter of the nanny. Who was I kidding anyway, thinking that he would want me? She decided that she wouldn't meet him. *Why should I allow him the opportunity to tell me how much he enjoyed leading me on?* She gulped back her tears. *He probably just wants to tell me what I am, and that he wants nothing to do with me,* Skylar thought as she could feel her heart seizing.

But despite her resolve, she knew she would go. In fact, she watched the clock, fearing she would be late. It didn't matter what happened. There was a chance, a small chance, that he really loved her. And deep inside Skylar knew that she loved Lander, and always would.

She got to the cottage garden early. Everything was in full bloom. Marigolds cascaded over the side of the raised flower gardens and tomatoes ripened on the vines. She sat in the chair on the back deck. It all seemed so familiar. She didn't realize that she was sitting in the chair her mother used to frequent, looking out on the memorable summer gardens. She watched a northern bluebird land on top of the colorful bird house. *What is it like to live such a simple, carefree life?* she wondered.

Things had gotten so complicated. *I love Lander, but I don't think he will ever forgive me for what I have done,* her heart cried. A white butterfly landed on one of the rose bushes and stirred a memory. She tried to reach the fleeting image, but it vaporized, escaping her. She could feel the pain in her chest as she thought of losing her mother, and now Lander. It seemed that everyone she loved disappeared from her life.

Lost in her thoughts, she was startled when the garden gate squealed open. He looked so handsome as he hesitated, looking at her. Then he smiled and it seemed to her that the entire world lit up. *Stop!* she thought. *It's over—once you confirm his fears he will want nothing to do with you.* She smiled weakly back, as he walked up to her and sitting in the chair opposite her, silently stared.

"I'm glad you want to talk," he said. "We've been avoiding each other for weeks now and we really need to straighten things out between us."

Looking away, Skylar blushed. *How can I talk about something I am so ashamed of?*

"Okay then, I'll start," Lander reached over and took her hand in his. "I am so sorry about Winnie. I was so stupid. I should have known that she was up to no good. When you saw her kiss me—it didn't mean anything!"

Winnie kissed him? Skylar looked into his eyes and knew that it was true. At first, her heart soared. He didn't love Winnie. But as the truth settled in, she could feel the tremendous weight of what it meant. She had reacted to a lie, but she had betrayed him. How could she tell him the truth of what happened that night? How could he ever forgive her?

She felt the blood rush from her face, and the dizziness made her head spin. Skylar just wanted to run—run away! Pulling her hand out of his she knew she couldn't disappear as she wanted to. *I have to tell him the truth. He deserves that much,* she thought. How can I tell him? How can I break his heart?

Lander's eyes opened wide as she pulled away from him. *She doesn't believe me,* he realized. *I can't let this happen. I have to convince her.* Standing before her, he reached down and pulled her toward him. Holding her in his arms, he cried, "I love you, don't you know how much I love you! It was a trick and I was so stupid I fell for it. Winnie and Lowell planned the whole thing!"

When the truth of the situation hit her she pulled away. *Oh my God! Lowell planned the whole thing! What am I going to do?* Turning away, she could feel the tears begin as the pain in her chest ached.

"Talk to me," Lander begged.

"I can't," she whispered, unable to look him in the eye.

She tried to pull away. She just wanted it all to end. It was too painful, unbearable. *How can I tell him what happened?*

"No—don't run away. Talk to me, nothing could be worse than the silence between us," Lander begged.

"Yes, it can. Don't you realize what happened?" she said as the tears poured down her face. "I thought you didn't love me. I was so alone and upset. I couldn't think and then he came!"

"Who? Who came?" Lander asked as he pulled back and stared.

"Lowell! Lowell came and he told me that you didn't love me, didn't want me. He came and comforted me—held me."

Skylar could hear the sharp inhalation of breath, as Lander's face paled.

"He made me feel safe, and wanted. And I thought you didn't want me. He wanted me." Skylar took a deep breath. She couldn't bear to look at him, as she finally blurted out the truth. "I slept with him!"

Skylar could hear his loud painful sigh as he let go of her. He seemed to collapse into the chair. It looked as if someone had punched him in the gut. His face registered pain and shock.

"I thought you knew! From the way you looked at me that morning, I thought that you had figured it out!" she shouted.

His face paled. Shaken, he looked away. "I suspected—from the way you looked, from the way your dress was rumpled. But I hoped...I hoped I was wrong," he whispered in a voice so beaten, so low, that her heart stopped.

She couldn't stand it. She couldn't stand to see the disappointment in his eyes. He had let her go, turned from her. Skylar couldn't breathe.

Turning, she ran. With tears blinding her —similar to the tears she spilt the night she spent with Lowell—she ran. Upon reaching her room, she locked the door and flopped on the bed. Putting the pillow over her head, she screamed. She didn't remember how long she had screamed or when she had fallen into a deep, mindless sleep. When she awoke to the morning light, Skylar only knew one thing. He hadn't come. He hadn't followed her.

The fool says in his heart, "There is no God." They are corrupt, doing abominable iniquity; there is none who does good. God looks down from heaven on the children of man to see if there are any who understand, who seek after God. They have all fallen away; together they have become corrupt; there is none who does good, not even one. Have those who work evil no knowledge, who eat up my people as they eat bread, and do not call upon God? There they are, in great terror, where there is no terror! For God scatters the bones of him who encamps against you; you put them to shame, for God has rejected them...
—Psalm 53: 1–6

Chapter Eighteen

At night, walking through darkened rooms we are afraid. We cannot see what is in front of us. Our step is unsure. Yet, we have been here before. We know the way—where everything is. Is it because we don't trust our memory? Can we forget that easily?

He has saved us. We know this. In the past, we have felt Him. He walked ahead of us. We learned to trust Him before. Is it because we don't trust our memories? Can we forget that easily?

Regina hung up the phone in disgust. *I let this go on too long!* she thought angrily. *I should have known enough to keep an eye on the little bastard!* Anthony Cole had been irate, screaming about Lowell. He had always mistrusted him. He had seen the way he looked at Winnie. He thought his daughter had more sense. On and on, he had complained.

"Today I opened the door to the back office, the one I was having renovated for her. And there he was – making love to my Winnie, Cole shouted. "I fired him on the spot. You better control him. I don't want him anywhere around my daughter. If you don't, I'll take steps—I'm warning you!"

Trying to calm him, Regina promised that she would take care of the matter. He was coming to talk to John tomorrow, and she knew she had to take control of the situation before it got out of hand. The last thing she wanted was Lander turning on Winnie. She had plans. She needed to get Lander and Winnie together. Lander could never learn of Winnie's indiscretion.

Picking up the phone, she called the dean of the college Lander was slated to attend. *Money is power,* she thought as the man interrupted his meeting to take her call. Winnie was just an average student, nothing special. She had to use all her power to convince him.

Shocked by her request, at first he refused. All of the spots had already been promised to other students. It wouldn't be fair, he claimed.

Regina chuckled at his naiveté. *Fair? Since when was the world fair?*

"I'm sure you could make room for the girl. She is the daughter of a very good friend and I would be extremely grateful." Listening carefully she could almost hear the tiny wheels of his greedy brain turning.

"And I'm sure that the new building I am planning to donate would give you even more room," she said—drawing him in.

"Well...for you, perhaps we could make an exception," the dean gulped.

"I thought you would see it my way. After all, the girl deserves a chance." She ended the call with a sense of victory.

Winnie will be going to college with Lander. That should seal the future nuptial, Regina thought. Now she would just have to take care of Lowell. He was mucking up her plans and no one was allowed to do that. Regina needed to take control.

*

Her stomach churned. Skylar was sure she had a touch of the flu.

She couldn't even brush her teeth, because the taste of the toothpaste brought on more nausea. It was an endless cycle each morning. She couldn't sit at the breakfast table—the smell of bacon repulsed her. She could see Bridget watching, worrying.

"I must have food poisoning," Skylar offered.

When a week went by and the queasiness didn't end, Bridget came to her room.

"I think you should see a doctor," she suggested.

"It's just a virus. It will pass," Skylar responded. But when the nausea continued past the second week, she acquiesced. Maybe the doctor would give her something to calm her nerves. Skylar was sure that it was nerves. Ever since she had told Lander the truth about her night with Lowell, she had been ill. She couldn't seem to cope with anything. She should have taken her driver's test to get her license, but she just didn't go. She didn't feel well enough. Skylar had been excited about driving but now she was listless, not caring about anything. Nothing seemed right since that evening. She couldn't get Lander out of her mind. The pain had never subsided. It had turned to an upset stomach. At times she felt dizzy, and thought she might faint. *It's my stomach. I can't eat and it's making me weak,* she decided. She wanted to keep busy—keeping her mind off Lander—but she had no energy.

Spending most of her late summer afternoons in her room didn't help. She didn't want to run into Lander. She had only seen him a few times since the meeting in the cottage garden, and he had ignored her. He was never home, as if he were avoiding her. Soon, he would be leaving for college and she might not see him for months. *It doesn't matter,* she thought. *He doesn't want me.* Nothing seemed to matter anyway. Skylar didn't know how she could go on living without him. She didn't really want to.

Sitting in the paper gown, as the doctor looked down her throat and in her ears, seemed a waste of time. She had just come to ease Bridget's mind. Skylar knew what was wrong with her. She had a broken heart and there was no medication on earth that could mend it again. *People are always saying that time mends a broken heart,* Skylar thought. She didn't believe it. Her heart was more than broken. It felt as if her heart had been torn from her chest. She was numb, knowing the pain of feeling again just might kill her.

After sending her to the office lavatory to give a urine sample, the doctor drew numerous tubes of blood from her arm.

"You can get dressed now," he instructed, nodding to Bridget and Skylar, "I'll meet you and your mother in my office with some findings."

Mother? If only I had a mother that I could talk to, Skylar thought. Bridget had gotten better in the last few years. She could speak now, although she didn't speak often. Lately she had treated Skylar like her own daughter—sharing her thoughts on a number of purely female topics. It was all new to Skylar, having grown up surrounded by men and boys. Regina despised her and ignored her. *It's always better when she ignores me,* she thought. *When she doesn't she is always belittling me.*

Bridget had gone shopping with her. It had been so special. Having someone truly care about what she would wear and how her hair was fixed meant so much. *And then I betrayed her trust and ruined the dress,* Skylar thought. *I betrayed one of her sons and slept with the other.* Sighing, she prayed that her real mother would guide her through this disaster.

The office was warmly paneled with dark wood, and the carpet was plush. Sitting in the leather chair in front of the intricately carved desk, Skylar watched as the elderly physician sat down.

Glancing momentarily at Bridget, he began: "Not all of the tests have come back of course, but I think I may know what is causing the nausea and fatigue."

Looking straight at Skylar in a no-nonsense manner, he continued, "You're not ill, young lady; you're pregnant."

At first she couldn't comprehend the words—they didn't make sense.

"No, that can't be..." Skylar's voice trailed off as she thought of the night with Lowell. The color drained from her face as the reality of her situation hit her.

"I'm afraid there is no doubt about it. I'll prescribe you some prenatal vitamins and something to alleviate the nausea. I'll also give you the name of a great obstetrician," he continued. "Now get some rest and the nausea should pass in a couple of weeks."

Bridget came and hooking her arm around Skylar's she helped the girl to her feet. Skylar's legs wobbled, as if they were rubber. The ride home in the car was silent, as she stared out the window the entire way. She was in shock. Bridget silently led her to her room. Skylar lay in a fetal position on her bed, her mind whirling in disbelief. *This is a nightmare! I know that I'll wake up soon.*

Finally, Bridget spoke. "Is it Lander's baby?"

"No—it's Lowell's," she heard herself respond. It was as if she were listening to a conversation from afar.

"Then you're going to have to tell him," Bridget answered softly as she stroked Skylar's arm.

"No, no...! I can't!" her mind screamed with fear as she felt the room closing in on her.

"He has the right to know. You have to give him the chance to do the right thing," Bridget answered, "For now just rest. You need to think, recover from the shock. I'm right across the hall if you need me."

Skylar didn't answer. Her mind was unfocused—unable to deal with the devastating news. *A baby?* Her hand reached down to hold her stomach. *Lowell's baby!* she wanted to scream. Instead, she wept. Whispering into her pillow, she cried, *Why isn't it Lander's baby?*

Her mind was fevered. She couldn't sleep. Softly rising, Skylar left her room. Walking gently, she didn't alert Bridget, who was across the hall, or any others in the house. She donned her coat and grabbed the keys to John's car. He had taken a plane out to a teacher's convention, and wasn't due home till late tonight. *He won't miss them,* she decided as she started the car and headed to an unknown destination. She just knew she needed to get away. She couldn't risk running into either Lowell or Lander. She didn't know what might happen if she did.

Cruising down Main Street, she didn't know what made her turn into the church parking lot. Gray-stoned and majestic, St Joseph's stood like a sentinel above the skyline of the small village. Entering through the massive wood door, she allowed her eyes time to adjust to the dim lighting. The soft candlelight was warm, making the large crucifix that hung over the center altar look life-like. Skylar walked up the aisle of the empty church and sat in the first pew. Her pain was palpable. She was beyond weeping. In silence, she questioned God. *How could you allow this to happen to me? You know I love Lander. What am I going to do?* her heart demanded.

Do you know what it is to be trapped? Do you have any idea? she continued.

I'm trapped by my body—trapped in a situation without a way out!

Suddenly she could feel a rage rising as anger penetrated her soul. Skylar looked up to accuse and was stuck dumb.

There He was. His kind eyes seemed to be looking at her. He looked as if He wanted to come to her, to hold her and comfort her. *The nails…*she realized. *He knows what it is like. Of course He does.*

She could feel the tears as they stung her cheeks.

"What am I to do?" she whispered out loud.

A sense of calm flowed over her. A feeling of peace permeated her heart. Bridget's words repeated in her mind. He has a right to know. Lowell needs to be given the opportunity to do the right thing.

Her longing for Lander rose. Skylar pushed it down. Looking at the crucifix, she saw the nails in his hands and feet. He couldn't move—he couldn't walk away.

Neither can I, Skylar decided. I can only do the right thing and leave it all in His hands.

She sat for hours, allowing the peace she felt to continue. She feared leaving His presence. Things seems so eternal here, so serene. She knew it couldn't continue this way, but she didn't want it to end. As the light that shone through the windows faded, she knew that it was getting late. *I have to find him. I have to tell him.*

She herself wasn't sure who she was talking about. It didn't matter. God would put him in her path. Leaving the church, Skylar was a different person. She was a believer, a mother.

*

She heard him laughing as soon as she entered the house. Sitting in the living room, he was on the phone. When she entered the room and sat down he was just hanging up. Smiling at her, he seemed interested.

"We have to talk," she told him.

"Sure, do you want to talk here?" Lowell asked, looking around to see if they were alone.

"Yes, let me tell you what you need to know before I lose my courage," she answered.

"You remember the night we spent together?" she continued.

"How could I forget?" he smiled, and rising, sat down beside her, wrapping his arm around her.

"Well, I'm pregnant," Skylar blurted out.

There was a pause. She couldn't look at him. She didn't want to know his reaction. After a few moments of silence, he lifted her chin and turned her head toward him.

"Don't worry. It's all going to be all right." Lowell kissed her tenderly on the cheek and then the lips.

Suddenly she felt safe, and let him hold her in his arms. Visions of Lander popped into her mind, but she pushed the thoughts away. She had to think of her baby. If Lowell was going to be a father, her baby deserved that.

"What are we going to do?" she asked.

"First, let's not tell anyone," he instructed.

"Bridget knows," she responded.

"That's okay. She will keep it to herself for now and by the time she tells everyone everything will be settled." He seemed insistent.

"Settled? What do you mean by settled?" Skylar asked.

Looking at her, his face softened. "Why, by then we will be married. You do want to marry me, don't you?"

In spite of her conflicting feelings, Skylar nodded yes.

"Then don't tell anyone. We don't want them to interfere. Go up to your room and pack a small bag. After everyone has gone to bed, sneak out. I've been summoned by the dragon lady for a meeting. Don't know what she wants, but after the meeting I will do a few errands to get things ready. I'll meet you at the bus station at midnight," he whispered.

Holding her close, he whispered in her ear, "Everything will be all right as long as you don't tell anyone. By the time the family finds out, we'll be married and everything will be okay."

He must love me, she realized. *Given all the choices, he is doing the right thing.*

His arms felt warm and protective. She tried to think of him as her friend—they had been friends all her life. Marriages had started and succeeded on less. *I will learn to love him,* she thought. *If he can do the right thing for the baby, so can I.*

Her heart cried for Lander, but her mind told her that Lowell was her future. She wasn't afraid any more. She felt that God was directing her steps. She would pack a bag. She would meet him and make everything right. Her baby wouldn't grow up without parents like she had.

He kissed her before he headed out the door. Skylar felt a sense of peace and headed to her room. She wanted to pack her bag and change her clothes, but most of all she didn't want to see Lander before she and Lowell were married.

> *The heart is deceitful above all things, and desperately sick; who can understand it?*
> —Jeremiah 17, 9

Chapter Nineteen

Our hearts are not necessarily connected to our minds, for love has little to do with logic. In our foolishness, we think we can control our feelings, deny the truth. We lie to ourselves more than we lie to those around us. When love is triggered, an ancient spirit moves us, and we cannot explain it. Love is often illogical, unexplainable, and painful. But as painful as love itself may be, the denial of that love is unbearable.

Lowell wasn't happy to be summoned by Regina. *The queen has sent out a decree,* he thought, as he entered her office. She sat behind her huge desk like an imperial. *Maybe she thinks she looks like a queen,* Lowell mused, *but she's just a shrunken old lady now!* He knew that she held all the purse-strings, so he smiled. He was curious about what she wanted. Sitting in the chair before her, he waited for her to reveal herself.

"Lowell," she croaked, "I know you and I haven't gotten along for many years."

As she paused, Lowell became wary.

"I am sorry that we never developed a closer relationship." Regina looked with feigned affection at her grandson. "I would like to make that up to you."

"In what way?" Lowell asked. He leaned forward, placing his elbows on her desk as his hands cradled his face. His casual pose seemed to annoy her. It pleased him to see the hatred she had always felt for him pass quickly over her face. Lowell held no illusions about her feelings.

She took on a false look of condescension. "I know that Lander is going away to college and that you were going to remain at home and attend the local college."

"Yes, what about it?" he answered. His sarcastic tone made Regina compress her lips as if trying to control her response.

"Well...I have decided that the local college is not good enough for one of my grandsons!" She smiled. "I've made a few calls and I'm sure you will be excited to learn that one of the most prestigious colleges has decided to take you on!"

"What college is that?" Lowell asked with a smirk.

"You're going to England!" Regina announced. "I managed to get in touch with an old friend of mine and you will be traveling to Europe. Imagine! All the wonders you will see. I bet you never expected such excitement."

Lowell smiled. "No, I would never expect you to go out of your way like this. It sounds wonderful!"

Regina couldn't hide her feeling of triumph. "You'll be leaving by the end of the week. I know it is short notice, but it shouldn't take you long to prepare. Of course, I will be giving you a generous credit line. You won't have to worry about anything.

She's trying to get rid of me. I wonder why? Lowell managed to grin. "England is cold in the winter. I'll need some money to buy new clothes. I can't thank you enough, Grandmother," Lowell responded as Regina had trouble not reveling in her presumed victory.

Rising, he watched as she wrote him a check for a thousand dollars. Tearing it from her checkbook, she looked up and handed it to him. "This should get you started. But remember, you'll have to be ready to leave by Friday."

Lowell promised to be ready and left the office. *She's really anxious to get rid of me. I wonder what she's up to...*he thought. Lowell had no intention of going to college. Why should he? He already had a corporation and millions to inherit. And the plans he had made for himself should cement his rights. Lander always liked school, but Lowell hated it. He hated anything that put him in a subservient position. Lowell had plans, big plans, and no one was going to stop him.

Looking at the check, he laughed. He was going right to the bank of issue to turn it into cash. *Just what I need,* he thought as he headed toward Skylar's room. Nothing was going to stop him from getting married. Not any surprising circumstances nor any old lady who was well past her prime. *She should be dead and buried already,* he thought as he softly knocked on Skylar's door. *Maybe she'll die of shock when she hears about the wedding!*

*

Skylar awoke from a light sleep when she heard him knocking at her door. She let him in her bedroom and closed the door so no one would see them together. She didn't want anyone, especially Lander, to suspect anything. She had been crying for hours. Drained and with a pounding headache, she had fallen asleep on her bed fully dressed. It was a shock to see Lowell, when she had been dreaming of Lander all through her nap. When she first heard the knocking, in the twilight of awakening she had even imagined it was Lander. He was coming to take her away, to marry her himself. In that dreamlike state, she dared to hope. Lowell put an end to that delusion.

"Are you packed?" Lowell asked, as he took her in his arms.

"No…not yet," she whispered.

"Well, hurry up. I want you to be ready at a moment's notice. I'm going out to prepare things, so you won't see me until you meet me at the bus station. Remember, don't let anyone know our plans," he instructed.

Skylar sighed, "I won't."

"I won't be at dinner. So I'm depending on you not to slip." He smiled as he turned to leave.

The mention of dinner made her stomach turn. The nausea hadn't subsided even though she had taken one of the pills that the doctor had prescribed. *I don't think I will be sitting at the dinner table anyway,* she thought as Lowell left—closing the door behind him.

True, she didn't have an appetite, but it was more than the nausea. As usual it was about Lander. If she went to dinner, he might be there. She had made up her mind. She would marry Lowell and make the marriage work. *I can't see Lander first,* her heart cried. *If I look into those eyes, I won't be able to do it!*

When Bridget called her for dinner, she told her that she was too nauseous to eat. Bridget had a tray with saltines and ginger ale sent up for Skylar. Nibbling on the crackers did settle her stomach. Pulling the overnight bag from under her bed, she packed a few days' worth of clothing. *How long will we be gone?* she wondered. There was too much time left—too much time to think. Every sound she heard in the hallway made her nervous. *Was Lander there? Was he so close?* Her heart beat quickly. She prayed that he would come, that he would tell her that he loved her. She knew it wouldn't happen. Even if he did she knew he would be horrified to learn that she was carrying his brother's baby. *It's hopeless,* she thought as she waited. Pulling out her rosaries, she prayed.

*

Regina smirked as Lowell, staring at the check, left her office. It had taken a lot of work but she had resolved all her problems. Lowell and Winnie would be thousands of miles apart. Winnie would be thrown in with Lander and hopefully, with a little encouragement, they would marry right after college. She had called in a lot of favors and committed lots of money to accomplish her goals but it was worth it.

She was going to get Anthony Cole's company! She had wanted it for years and it would make her one of the richest women in the country. *He had a lot of nerve yelling at me!* she thought with aggravation. And she knew that in the end he would pay for the mistake. No one talked to her that way. Everything was set and once the marriage of Lander and Winnie combined the two giants, she would teach Anthony Cole a lesson he would never forget.

Now she had just one more loose end—Skylar! *I have to get rid of her.* She decided that once the twins were away she would find a way to get her out. She didn't ever want to see her again. She almost ruined everything and she certainly doesn't belong here. *I'll figure that out later,* she decided.

Grabbing the folded newspaper on her desk, Regina quickly scanned the front page and opened it, hoping to see the business section. Instead she caught the obituaries, and immediately his picture caught her eye. Her heart stopped, then quickened when she saw his face. There was no mistaking who it was. Daniel, her Daniel, was staring out at her. Although the photo was of an older version of him, there was no mistaking the ruggedly handsome face that haunted her dreams. *Oh my God!* Regina realized. *He's gone!*

The short obit told the story of his life. *Predeceased by his wife of twenty-one years—so he had been alone! I could have gone to him!* Her eyes hungered for more. He had married a fellow teacher and had five children. The article stated that Daniel had been a beloved high school teacher since graduation from college, still living in the little town she had once belittled. He had seven grandchildren! Sighing, Regina stared at his photo. He was still as handsome as he had been in college. She could feel the tears start. They surprised her. *Why am I crying?* she wondered.

It hit her hard. As long as Daniel was alive, she had a small hope, a hope that was hidden deeply in her heart. *I would have never done it!* she knew. Yet, as long as he was in this world, she had felt that maybe….just maybe. Now there would never be that chance, no matter how remote. She could never go to him now. He was gone. Regina knew that she would have never reached out, never admitted that she still loved him. She knew that her pride would never allow her to call him or even write to him. Still, as long as he was alive there was always that hope, that secret dream still alive in her heart.

Now it's too late, she thought as she stared at his photo. Now I will never see him again. She wondered if he had been happy. *Did he ever think of me?* she mused. In all the years that had passed, she had never been able to forget him. As decades passed she grew to realize that true love never dies. Without him her heart had been empty. Regina had tried to fill that empty spot up with money. When money didn't satisfy, she had clung to power. But the only power that counted, the power to have Daniel in her life, escaped her. In the end, he had been all that mattered. It had taken Regina a lifetime to know that. Now it didn't matter what she knew. She would never see him again.

Folding the paper so his picture was facing out, she placed it in her top drawer. Leaning back in her chair, she closed her eyes and allowed the sorrow to wash over her. She hadn't felt such pain since the day she left him. She had never really grieved when Harrison died. *Oh I felt bad, but not like this,* she remembered.

Now, with Daniel gone, Regina felt as if her soul had been torn from her body. Her chest burned in the spot where it had been forcibly removed. *How can I be in the world without him?* her heart cried. Time had passed too quickly. Somehow, she had always felt that he would come to her. At night she had dreamt that he, missing her as much as she missed him, had come to her. Tugged by the string that connected the two hearts, he had appeared on her doorstep. He begged her to take him back. He promised to live whatever lifestyle she wanted.

That loving reunion had never happened. She had forced herself to stay away from him. At times, the separation had been unbearable. However, as the years rolled away it became impossible go to him. *Did he ever love me as much as I loved him?* she thought. Somehow she doubted it. If he had he would have come to her. She had barely kept herself from him. In the very beginning, she thought he would change his mind. Regina hoped that without her, he would have realized that she was right. He would have realized that wasting away in a small town on a small salary was no way to live. She waited. She waited until the day she found Harrison.

Maybe if I had gone to him then? She wondered if it would have made a difference. Would he have come back to her? Or would she have accepted his way of life? *Oh, how I wish I had gone with him!*

The thought startled her. Could she have been happy as a school teacher's wife? Would being in his arms each night have made up for the lack of wealth? *Now, I'll never know,* she sighed. Opening the top drawer, she stared at the face of the only man she would ever love. Wealth and security had come at a high price, a price that had been too much to pay. The waiting game was over. He was gone and she would never hold him in her arms, never inhale the scent of him. She remembered the way she would sniff his coat before she gave it to him. His scent lingered. His memory lingered. And now memories were all she could have. The choice was no longer hers.

She felt her shoulders relax, her muscles ease. It was as if she had been steeling herself for years to resist him. Now, with the decision out of her control, she could let go.

Or can I? she thought. *I wonder if, in a few months, I can go to his grave. Maybe I can give him some flowers. Maybe there I can tell him how much I love him?* she thought.

*

Bridget was afraid she was going to have to eat alone. Lander hadn't come home, and Lowell was nowhere to be seen. Skylar was too ill to eat. She prayed her mother wouldn't join her. Despite the fact that she hated to eat alone, she dreaded spending any one-on-one time with her mother.

She was both happy and surprised when John arrived. They could share an intimate and much deserved meal alone. She knew that she had to tell him about Skylar's pregnancy and Lowell's responsibility for it. *Not now!* she decided. *I don't want to hit him with all the bad news just as he gets home.* She decided to tell him that night, or maybe even tomorrow. The problems weren't going away, and there was no need to include him in the worries immediately.

Sitting across from him, she could feel the love between them. They had been through so much over the years, but it had just made the bond between them stronger. Reaching over, she touched his hand and he responded with a loving grip. His smile dazzled. *I think he's gotten even handsomer over the years.* There was a time, deep in her depression, when she was sure she was going to lose him. She could see the feelings that Hannah tried to hide whenever he was around. It had only made her depression deepen. *So why couldn't I reach out to him?* she thought. *The more I wanted him, needed him, the more I withdrew.*

Looking across the table, it hit her. She had been angry, so angry at him. He had brought her back to this house—back to the domineering mother she had managed to escape. It had taken Bridget all the strength in her spirit to deny her mother's wishes and marry John. Her mother had groomed her to marry Anthony Cole, but Bridget loved John. *A mere teacher,* she thought, *a teacher who had nothing to offer but himself and his love.* But what a love it had been. The love had carried them through illness and separation. It had been strong enough to carry them through living with Regina. *But now it is time to leave,* she thought.

She would talk to him about it. Tonight, she would let him know that it was time to leave and create a new life, a home of their own. As she looked across the table, and listened to the details of his conference, she knew that while she would miss her sons, it was time. Time to start a new life, the life they should have had from the beginning. That is the conversation they would have tonight. The troubles could wait until tomorrow—tonight was about joy.

Keep your heart with all vigilance, for from it flow the springs of life.
—Proverbs 4: 23

Chapter Twenty

The heart is a delicate organ. Able to soar with joy or plunge into despair, it rules the pivotal moments of our life. Yet the heart is often mistaken, unable to see the truth. We allow our heart to rule us with fear, lies, or misunderstandings.

It is in those emotional moments we should turn to the God who created our heart. He knows the twists and turns that the human heart can take. Only He can guide us through the labyrinth of passion that clouds our reasoning.

Dressed in a silk skirt and her best blouse, Skylar waited. She waited for the house to grow silent. She heard Regina, as was her habit, go to bed early. She listened as John and Bridget laughingly entered their room across the hall, and prayed that Bridget hadn't told him yet. Just in case Bridget had told him, she waited. She knew that once John found out about her pregnancy, he would want to talk to her. When he didn't knock on her door, she guessed that Bridget was waiting to tell him. *Maybe she is waiting until she knows what Lowell's response is,* Skylar thought as she combed her blond curls into a pony tail.

The house remained quiet. Skylar could hear the grandfather clock ticking in the hall. Lander hadn't come home, and she was thankful. The last thing she wanted was to see him. It was only ten, but she couldn't sit around anymore. She felt so closed in. It felt like the walls were moving in, ready to squeeze her to death. *I have to get out of here,* she decided. *I've made up my mind and there is no point waiting around.*

Skylar softly opened her bedroom door and gently closed it. She didn't want anyone looking into her room and noticing that it was empty. In velvet slip-on shoes that she had picked deliberately she stepped gingerly down the hallway. Past the only parents she had ever known. Past the woman who had made her childhood miserable. Past Lander's bedroom with her breath catching in her throat. *Is he in there?* she wondered, even though she hadn't heard him come in.

She wanted to go to him. *If I tell him how much I love him it might not matter,* she dreamed. Pulling herself together she dismissed the ridiculous thought. Clutching her duffel bag, she slipped down the stairs. Closing the front door, she quietly locked the deadlock. The warm air was sweet with the smell of summer flowers. *The walk will do me good,* she decided as she headed toward the bus station. Tonight her new life would begin. She would give her child his parents—a gift she had never received.

The bus station was busy and filled with people. The large wall clock struck the eleventh hour as she found herself a secluded spot on the long wooden bench along the far wall. It would be an hour before he came, she realized as she sat back. Taking deep breaths she tried to relax. Her life, as she knew it, was about to end. She would soon be a wife and a mother. Her dreams would no longer be just about herself.

She watched a young couple, clearly newlyweds, as they snuggled on the opposite bench. It was as if they were in a bubble, with no one around them. *They only see each other,* she thought, as she watched them stare into each other's eyes. Skylar wondered if it would be that way for Lowell and her. Would they ever be so in love that nothing or nobody else would matter? Even now, on the eve of their wedding, Skylar had her doubts. She was surprised when Lowell asked her to marry him. She had always thought that he really loved Winnie, ever since she had caught them together in the hallway of the locker room. Now, she doubted that Lowell loved anyone. *So why marry him?* she thought. *Because he is the father of my child,* she answered herself, touching her abdomen unconsciously.

She watched as the minutes ticked away. The young couple left, his arm draped over her shoulder. On their way home for her to met his family, she overheard, as they headed out west. The clock struck midnight as they disappeared into the Greyhound bus. *Lowell should be here any minute,* she thought as she scanned the large luggage-lined room for any sight of him. *He's always late,* Skylar thought, shrugging off any fear of him not showing. She wondered where he planned to take her. Somewhere they could get married without many questions about their age, she was sure.

Skylar tried to push all fear aside, and looked at the bus schedule posted on the moving electronic sign above the ticket stations. In the next few hours, there were buses going to California, Ohio, Virginia, and Florida. She had never traveled. Never been away from the only home she had ever known. Despite her misgivings, she was a little excited about starting out on a whole new adventure. There were so many things in the world that she would like to see.

But I'd rather see them with Lander. The thought rose so suddenly. She pushed it away. *I have to stop thinking of him,* she decided. Looking at the clock she realized that it was now half-past midnight and still there was no sign of Lowell. She checked her cell, but there were no messages. Looking around, she watched as a toddler rocked her baby doll in her arms. The tiny girl sat with her brother and parents. The older brother was playing with toy trucks, rolling them along the bench while the father checked the bus schedule and the mother seemed lost in her romance novel. *A family,* she thought. *Do they even know how special they are, or do they just take each other for granted?* She watched as the father grabbed the little girl's hand and the mother directed the boy to pick up his toys. Heading out to the bus, they were on their way home—to Ohio.

The clock struck one with a loud gong that aroused some of the sleepers in the room. One older man smiled as his daughter arrived from college and ran to his arms. It wasn't a happy reunion. Apparently someone had passed away and she was home for the services. They left for the parking lot and disappeared into the dark night. *He's an hour late,* Skylar thought as she felt herself yawn. Her eyes were heavy—it had been a long day. She would just close them for a minute, she decided. Lowell would see her sitting here when he came. *Just for a minute,* she thought as the world around her disappeared.

It was three fifteen when she awoke. At first she couldn't remember where she was. Looking around, it came back to her. She had been dreaming about Lander. *Where is Lowell?* she wondered looking around. The bus station was almost empty now. Just one ticket station was open and an old man dozed on the bench across the room. The sign announcing the future departures was less busy. Just two buses—one for Georgia and one for Florida, were scheduled in the next hour. Rubbing her eyes, she started to panic. *What if he changed his mind? What if he's not coming?* Skylar was embarrassed. Should she go home? *No,* she decided, *I can't go home with my tail between my legs.* Looking at the bus schedule she decided that if he didn't come, she would have to leave without him.

I don't have enough money, she realized. He couldn't just leave her here. Something must have happened. She decided to keep waiting. She couldn't face going home. She couldn't face the shame of her pregnancy and Lowell's rejection. She couldn't face her father and Lander when they found out. *He'll come,* she thought as she crossed her arms to ward off the cold of the empty station. *He wouldn't just leave me like this!* she decided.

Skylar heard the clock strike five, as she dozed off again. The noise that was now filling the station aroused her. Excited people headed for vacations, business men headed for meetings, and college students headed for freedom started to crowd the station, waiting for their early morning departures. Skylar knew now. He wasn't coming. She didn't know what to do. She sat there—purely out of habit—unable to make the move toward home. *What am I going to do?* she wondered as she sat frozen in despair. She wished she could just disappear.

Looking up she saw John Laverty. Weaving his way through the crowd, he sat beside her. Without a word, he took her hand in his.

For a few minutes he just sat, allowing her to adjust to the truth.

"Are you ready to come home?" he asked, squeezing her hand.

"Yes," was all she could manage.

She allowed him to take her bag and lead her toward the car in the lot. She hoped that no one was staring. She hoped it looked as if the person she had been waiting for arrived. Skylar wouldn't look at the ticket station. She imagined the old man was wondering why she was leaving without boarding a bus. *It doesn't matter,* she decided, *my baby and me are alone. No one is coming.*

The ride home was quiet. She was grateful for that, happy that he didn't question her or spurn her for the pregnancy. She was sure now that Bridget had told him. Why else would he have come for her? She was grateful to have a place to go. How long the mansion would be her home was something she wondered about. But it was something for another day.

Bridget was waiting and folded her in her arms as soon as she stepped in the door.

"I found her at the bus station. He wasn't with her," said John as he carried her suitcase in behind her.

"How did you know where I was?" Skylar whispered.

"He left a note on his pillow," Bridget answered. "He left a note saying that he was going away to be married."

Skylar's heart soared. "Where is he then? He never came! Is he all right?"

Bridget pulled back, and holding Skylar by both shoulders answered, "He's all right. He just called and said that he would be home soon. He said we would all understand when he got home—he would explain it all then."

Looking over Bridget, Skylar could see Lander standing on the staircase. He was staring at her. She wanted to run, but there was no place to go.

"Does Lander know about the baby?" she asked Bridget.

"No," she answered, "I think that you should be the one to tell him."

Skylar prayed silently. This was her worst nightmare. She could hear his footsteps approaching, but she couldn't look up. Shame filled her as she thought of telling him about the baby. *I can't do it!* she panicked. Then she felt his hand take hers.

A thrill ran through her like a bolt of electricity when the warmth of his touch aroused her from her fear. He drew her with him and she silently followed as he led her to the sofa. Sitting, he pulled her down beside him. Yet, still she couldn't bring herself to look at him.

"Skylar, what is going on around here?" Lander asked.

She gulped, trying to find the right words. Looking up into those kind green eyes was more then she could bear. Staring into the face of the one she truly loved started the tears. Unable to say a word, Skylar sobbed. And the harder she cried the tighter Lander held her.

"Sh...It will be all right," he whispered softly as he stroked her hair. "There is nothing so bad that we can't work through it together."

"You don't know! You don't understand," she cried feeling as if her heart would break through her chest.

Pulling back, and looking away, Skylar decided to get it over with. "I'm in trouble!"

"What kind of trouble?" Lander asked.

"I'm pregnant!" she blurted out.

The silence filled the room and chilled her soul. She didn't want to look at him, but just had to. All the color had drained from his face. She had never seen him so shaken. He stared at her and she withered under his gaze.

After minutes that seemed like an eternity, he asked, "Who is he?"

Looking away, Skylar hung her head. With a sigh, she responded, "Lowell, the father is Lowell. We were supposed to run away and marry, but he never came. He left a note that he was running away to get married but he never came to meet me at the bus station."

He remained quiet, his breathing heavy. Skylar couldn't bear the silence. It became oppressive, like a heavy blanket. She couldn't breathe.

"It was that night—prom night!" she said. "I never meant...."

Looking at him, she wondered as he looked away. He looked pale and confused. She wanted to reach out and touch his cheek. She wanted to tell him that the night with Lowell didn't mean anything. But he looked so distant, so cold.

It's over, she suddenly knew. *Any chance we may have had is over.* He can't even look at me—I've disappointed him so deeply. She could feel the heat of shame rising to her cheeks. She couldn't bear for him to think of her this way. She was about to bolt out of the room and up the stairs when Bridget and John entered with a tray. *Coffee and scones to fill the empty stomach,* thought Skylar, *but nothing to fill the empty soul.*

She couldn't stay. Excusing herself, she ran up the stairs. Her legs felt heavy and she was weary. She was tired of life and all the pain she had caused. Lying in her bed, the bed she had left with such hope the evening before, she found she couldn't even cry. Tumbling into an exhausted sleep, Skylar dreamed of a different life. A dream she wouldn't remember when she awoke.

Do not be unequally yoked with unbelievers. For what partnership has righteousness with lawlessness? Or what fellowship has light with darkness? What accord has Christ with Belial? Or what portion does a believer share with an unbeliever? What agreement has the temple of God with idols? For we are the temple of the living God; as God said, "I will make my dwelling among them and walk among them, and I will be their God, and they shall be my people. Therefore go out from their midst, and be separate from them, says the Lord, and touch no unclean thing; then I will welcome you, and I will be a father to you, and you shall be sons and daughters to me, says the Lord Almighty."
—*2 Corinthians 6, 14-18*

Chapter Twenty-One

We live in the world, but Christ tells us that we are not of this world. And many who share this world are not of the same spirit. In a world that calls evil good and good evil, it is only the discerning heart that knows the difference. And it is only through prayer that discernment is gifted.

Men crucified Him because they could not bear to have good walk the earth. Good is too dazzling—it hurts our eyes. The light is uncomfortable, unnerving. By glowing it deepens the darkness around it. If they are celebrating you, and you feel contented and loved, perhaps you are walking in the shade.

Skylar awoke to the sound of shouting. By the dim light that filtered in through her window she knew that it was evening. *I've been sleeping all day,* she realized. Rising, she donned her robe and went to the bathroom to wash. The sleep had acted like a tonic. She showered and felt the hot water revive her cold, tired body. Refreshed, she donned a comfortable sweat suit and tied her damp hair up in a bun. Looking in the mirror she was surprised. She no longer looked shaken and pale. Her color was back and she was determined to face the world with courage and honesty.

Slipping down the stairs, she was stunned to see John Laverty shouting at someone in the living room. She had never seen him so angry. Bridget held his arm and looked as if she were trying to calm him. *Who's in the living room?* she wondered as she entered the hall. Turning, John looked at her. His face fell, defeated and beaten.

"What is it?" she asked as she saw the sympathy in Bridget's eyes. Walking into the living room, she saw him. Lowell was sitting on the couch, his arm around Winnie. Glancing back at John, she didn't know what to do. John came and placed his arm around her, as if to steady her. Looking away, she could see Lander standing in the corner—staring at her. It was too much to take in. Skylar felt confused. *Why is Lowell just sitting there?* she wondered. *What is Winnie doing here?*

Looking back, she could see the wariness on Lowell's face as he stared at her. He seemed unsure. Unsure of what the others knew about Skylar's condition.

"Hi Skylar," he said, as he stared at her. "I'm afraid you walked in on a family argument. My father seems upset that I'm with Winnie."

Looking around, she could feel all eyes on her. She could feel her heart stop as she watched Lowell lean over and kiss Winnie on her cheek. *He's with her?* she thought, looking over at Lander, who stared at the floor.

Suddenly a door slammed and Regina appeared in the hall. "What is going on here? Can't I get any peace in my own house?"

Looking around, Regina stared at Winnie and Lowell. "What is this? What's going on here?!"

Lowell rose with a wide grin. "I don't understand it, Granny! You'd think that my father would be happy. Nobody wants to congratulate me."

"Congratulate you for what?" Regina retorted.

"Why, on my marriage!" Lowell laughed. "Winnie and I are husband and wife."

"No…that's impossible!" shouted Regina. Lowell and Regina stood staring at each other.

"It's true!" Lowell smiled. "We were married last night. We took the train down to Maryland and tied the knot."

"No!" shouted Regina as she turned her attention to Winnie. "You were supposed to marry Lander!"

Winnie, appearing a little shaken by the strong reaction, remained mute.

Skylar stood silently. She could feel her body tremble as a sense of the surreal overcame her. *He ran away and married her. While I was waiting for him in the bus station, he was marrying Winnie?*

She could feel her knees buckling as the truth of what was happening hit her. John held on. If he wasn't holding her, she knew she would collapse.

"Come Skylar," John whispered. "Let's go into the kitchen and sit."

Skylar followed him willingly. She could hear the shouting and anger that escalated behind her but it didn't seem to matter. *He betrayed me,* she realized as Bridget put the kettle on for tea.

Nothing mattered now. The time for arguments was over. Lowell had married Winnie, and Skylar was left with nothing. *Nothing but his baby,* she reminded herself.

They could hear the shouting muffled by the closed kitchen door, but everyone in the kitchen seemed to whisper. It was as if the soft voices could soften the blow that Skylar was feeling. She felt as if she had been punched in the stomach. The pain was so severe that she could think of nothing else. She knew that John and Bridget loved her, but they couldn't stop the pain. No one could stop the pain.

Lander had followed them into the kitchen and sat beside Skylar. He took her hand and held it tight.

Looking up at his parents, he said, "Can you leave us alone for a minute? I have to talk to Skylar alone."

It was the first time she had heard his voice since she had told him about her pregnancy. *I can't,* she thought. *I can't sit here and let him tell me what a disappointment I am.* Before she could speak, John and Bridget left the room. Skylar couldn't look at Lander. She tried to pull her hand from his, but he seemed intent on keeping the connection.

"Skylar, are you all right?" he whispered.

She could feel the tears starting. *I can't speak now. If I speak I'll lose control.*

He stood up and gently pulling her up, he held her in his arms.

"Don't you know," he murmured, his voice husky with emotion, "don't you know how much I love you?"

Skylar couldn't believe her ears. *What is he saying?*

Pulling back, he looked at her. Skylar looked away. Shame filled her.

"Say something," he pleaded.

"It's too late," she whispered. "It's too late for us."

"Why are you saying that?" Lander asked, as he continued to hold her.

"The baby—Lowell's baby!" she cried.

"It's not Lowell's baby. Lowell gave up any right to that baby when he married Winnie," he said. "It's your baby, and if it is yours then it is mine. I will love him and raise him as my own."

Skylar was shocked. He guided her to sit in the chair. Kneeling before her, he took both of her hands in his.

"Will you marry me?" he asked.

Looking into his eyes—those kind green eyes—Skylar felt as if she were in a dream. *If this is a dream I hope I never wake up!*

"Yes," was all she could say.

Smiling, he rose and gently pulled her to her feet. Drying her tears with a tissue, he pulled her closer and kissed her gently.

Pulling back, he continued, "Well, let's go tell the others."

*

The fight between Regina and Lowell had escalated. Lander, with his arm around Skylar, entered the living room only to hear Regina shouting.

"I will get it annulled! You know the pull I have," she spit and Lowell laughed.

"We are married and you can't get it annulled without our cooperation," Lowell continued. "Besides, I would think you would be happy that one of your grandsons married into the Cole family. Isn't that what you always wanted?"

"You won't get a dime from me! I'll cut you off!" Regina retorted.

"You don't seem to understand. I don't need your money any more. I have my wife's money now and we plan to have a good time with it," Lowell answered.

Winnie seemed confused. She had never expected this reaction. Regina had always gone out of her way to befriend Winnie. *I've never seen her like this,* she thought as she watched the fireworks.

"Why are you upset?" Winnie finally spoke up.

Regina turned from Lowell and gave Winnie a withering glare. "You were supposed to marry Lander. He's the one I groomed for you!"

"Oh, so it isn't Winnie that bothers you," Lowell answered. "It's me that you object to. You had plans for the 'crown prince,' did you not?"

Lander finally spoke up. "I never was going to marry Winnie anyway. I'm going to marry Skylar. I love her."

Regina froze, and then collapsed into the wing chair. "I don't believe this! This is my house. How did things get so out of control?"

It took her a moment to regain her composure. "I will not allow this. Lander—you will marry Winnie. I will have this marriage annulled."

Turning toward Skylar, she spit, "And you—you will get out of my house. You were never welcome here and I should have tossed your mother out before you were born!"

Lander tightened his grip on Skylar. "No, Granny, she has always belonged, and as my wife—she will be welcomed wherever I am welcomed."

In the moment of silence that followed, Bridget walked down the stairs in her coat and carrying a bag. Regina was shocked—it reminded her of the day she left to marry John.

"Lowell, we are leaving—are you coming with us?" Bridget announced.

Lowell looked up and laughed. "Why would I go with you? Granny just needs a little time to get used to the idea that I am the important grandson now. Don't you Granny?"

Bridget looked at John. "It's time now."

John smiled. "Lander, Skylar, get your things. We'll be leaving now."

"Leaving?" Regina rose. "Where do you think you are going? You're not taking Lander with you!"

"It's time for me to go," Lander responded, walking over to his grandmother and giving her a kiss on her cheek.

"No!" she shouted. "I will not allow it!"

It took Lander and Skylar just a few minutes to pack their possessions. Walking out the front door, John smiled at the setting sun. It painted the sky a golden orange. He felt free, as if a heavy weight had been lifted from his back. He and Bridget had been planning to leave for the last few months. They had purchased a small ranch on the other side of town, close to the school John taught in. The right moment had come and the burning light of the sunset seemed a sign confirming their decision.

"Isn't it beautiful?" Bridget smiled as she stepped off the front porch.

John, turning to close the door to the mansion, watched as Regina turned to look at Lowell. She narrowed her eyes, and licked her lips.

"It's more beautiful than you realize," he smiled as he closed the door.

About Author
Karen Kelly Boyce

Karen is best known for her series of novels which are based on the graces of the Rosary. *In the Midst of Wolves* is her fourth novel. *According to Thy Word, Into the Way of Peace,* and *Down Right Good* have all received the Seal of Approval from the CWG and *Down Right Good* has won the Eric Hoffer award for commercial fiction. She is a weekly columnist on the Catholic Writer's Guild Blog.

All of Karen's books are available on www.amazon.com

With the birth of her grandchildren, Conner and Kaitlyn, Karen has written a series of children's books. *The Sisters of the Last Straw* series is published by Chesterton press and is available at www.chestertonpress.com

Made in the USA
Monee, IL
18 March 2025